— Beverly Hills Butler —

By the same author

Rocking the Boat

— Beverly Hills Butler —

IAN ROSS

HEINEMANN : LONDON

William Heinemann Ltd
Michelin House, 81 Fulham Road, London SW3 6RB

LONDON MELBOURNE AUCKLAND

First published 1991
Copyright © Ian Ross 1991

A CIP catalogue record for this book
is available from the British Library
ISBN 0 434 65276 8

Printed and bound in Great Britain
by Clays Ltd, St Ives plc

'Man walketh in a vain shadow, and disquieteth himself in vain: he heapeth up riches and cannot tell who shall gather them.'

Psalm xxxix.7

— Prologue —

'This is the end, Paul!'

My wife Natasha sat on a packing case in what had been the living room. Imprints left behind in dust on the walls and on the marble mantelpiece were all that remained to remind us that until today this had been our home.

I hadn't even been much use packing up. I couldn't face it. My books, my records – what would become of them? Natasha soldiered through it all, organising the children and the nanny, lifting and heaving, shoving and folding, the packing cases piling up, her energy carried her over her grief. But now everything we were taking with us was packed. The floors of a five-storey house, each one a cog in the family wheel, were littered with the residue.

'Don't say that!' I moved near her. 'Things will be OK.' The disaster was so large, so impossible to embrace, it made it easier to deny. It just couldn't be happening. We would soon wake up. 'Come on, Natasha . . .' I ventured an arm around her huddled shoulders. They were hard and cold, like thin points of rock, broken by the impossible tide.

'Get away from me!' The mainspring of her grief uncoiled and flailed at me furiously. She let out a sob. 'What's going to happen to us?' Her face, white and tired, was streaked with dirt, streaked with tears. She drew a hand across it. Her hands were thin and strong like the rest of her. Her hair was frizzed out like a gypsy's, her sweater and jeans filthy, her ankles bare above her black moccasins. I could see the bulge of her small breasts under the sweater. Her tears made me feel incongruously horny. I approached her again. 'Come on, pet . . .' I was chuckling. I couldn't help it. This time I held her. She was like an iron rail. She said, 'How could you do this to us? The children?'

'I was trying to make things better – '

'That's what you always say.'

'Things always come right, don't they?'

'Not this time.'

'Come on Natasha. Don't be negative.'

'*Negative?* You've lost our home! We're bankrupt!'

'Tell it not in Gath!'

'What?'

'It's just a quote. David's Lament. I couldn't help thinking of it.'

'I'm sick of your stupid quotes!'

'"*I'm* homeless. You've got somewhere.'

'You can come too. We've told you that.'

I shook my head. We had been through this. Something else I couldn't face. Natasha and the children were going to live with her mother, in Sussex. The house, a minor stately, was large. Large enough to encompass this emergency. Not large enough, though, for her mother and me. Nowhere could be. Under her roof, on her terms, being constantly reminded of my failings, so many in my mother-in-law's eyes, even more than in my wife's. Exposed, impotent and emasculated before my children. I shuddered. I couldn't do it. Only murder could ensue. Stripped of my cover I must run and hide. But where?

The doorbell rang. I looked around. I'd never realised how much I liked the place. The cornices – I'd never even noticed them before.

Natasha went to the door. I heard her mother in the hall.

'Darling . . .'

'Mummy . . . oh, God!'

'I've brought Nigel to help. Someone strong . . .'

I felt the shock, like a blow. Things had been bad. Natasha's mother, true to form, had managed to make them worse. Nigel Banstead lived near her in the country in a gloriously moated Elizabethan jewel that had housed so many generations of Bansteads before him. He and Natasha had grown up together. How deep their friendship through childhood and adolescence had been, how far it had gone, was something Natasha clammed up moodily about whenever I quizzed her.

Nigel had another house, another gem, in a small, quiet street off Eaton Square. At thirty-five, my age, he was a director of a well-known merchant bank, the youngest on the board, ruthless, brilliant and popular. The major disappointment of Natasha's marriage, from her mother's point of view, was that it was not the fine upstanding figure of Nigel who stood beside her daughter at the altar. But Nigel had never married. Seen and reported in the gossip columns though he often was, with a succession of adoring beauties at Annabel's, he had never succumbed. Too busy, too dedicated to the bank, perhaps.

The door opened, I stared wildly about. There was no escape. Nigel entered the room, exuding self-assurance and sympathetic bonhomie.

'How's the boy?' The hand he held out to me in quiet sympathy was firm, soft, signet-ringed, beautifully maintained. Dark hairs on the reddish wrist showed below two perfect inches of snowy cuff which protruded from the tailored sleeve of a chalk-stripe suit – a masterpiece of exquisite understatement. He wore a maroon silk handkerchief in his breast pocket, an old Etonian tie. His voice like his hair was rich and dark, measured, calm, modulated with resonances that only generations of English breeding can bestow.

'Not too bad, I suppose.' I felt worn and torn and grossly inferior.

'All things considered, eh?' If he'd offered me a job at the bank, making tea or something, the job my mother-in-law was always on about, I'd have jumped at it then and there. But he didn't.

'Never mind. You'll think of something. You always do.'

He looked around and rubbed his hands briskly. 'Everything set?'

'I suppose so, yes.'

'I told Lady Roxbury I'd drive everyone down in my car.'

'Jolly decent of you.'

'The least I could do in the circs. How about you? Are you coming along? It's a bit of a squash in the Rolls.'

'No, no. I'll wait for the removal men. Got a lot to organise.'

'Of course you have. And then what?'

'Well, as you said, I'll think of something. I always do.'

'Of course you will. Going to base yourself in Sussex?' Nigel spoke with careful nonchalance.

I eyed him guardedly. 'I don't know. I doubt it.'

Lady Roxbury called from the hall, 'Come along, everybody . . .' Children were tumbling down the stairs, voices of all ages tumbling over voices. Excitement, mystery, confusion.

'Hurry up!' Events were overtaking life. Things were moving too fast. I went out to the hall. It was already empty. 'Come along, Daddy . . .' They were climbing all over Nigel's car.

I stood by one of the doors. Expensive leather rushed around my face. I breathed it in, the stranger at the feast. It was rich and warm. The children's faces were red and happy with adventure. Lady Roxbury's face, smiling, looked back at me from the front seat, wrapped in fur, a red gash in the chalky mask, hair set hard, like nylon. 'Will you be able to *manage* dear?'

'Yes, yes.'

'With the *men*, I mean.'

'Of course I will.'

Natasha appeared beside me, up against the car door, the last to board. Her face was set, like a wild, hunted animal. I looked into it, searching out the hate and the love. I heard myself saying the same, empty words: 'Don't worry, darling. I'll think of something . . .'

She said, 'I don't know, Paul. If you don't do something soon, I don't know if I – '

'Natasha!' The cry came up from the forest of time. I pulled her face against mine. Her mouth was hard and unyielding, full of the salty slime of despair.

— I —

'Business or pleasure?'

'I'm sorry?' I surfaced from my jet-lagged reverie. From behind thick glass the immigration officer repeated his question, this time with patient emphasis.

'The purpose of your visit, sir. Business or pleasure?' He held my passport in his hands, like a hostage. Rifling through the pages, glancing from my photo to my face, this was a man who took nothing for granted, who had seen humanity streaming by, like cattle, on its hopeless trail of dreams.

'A bit of both, I hope.' Once woken I was breezy. He studied me with mounting interest. His black tie was shiny like the streaks of hair plastered either side of his white skull. Official strip light shone in beads of sweat over his corrugated brow. The line behind me shifted its feet.

'Ya godda B1 only visa.'

'Is that a problem?'

'If you intend working.'

'Oh, well, just pleasure then.'

'How ya gonna live?'

'Rather well, I hope.'

He folded my passport in his two hands and watched me over it, mantis-like, for several moments.

'Before I allow you to enter the United States I need to know how you intend supporting yourself. Where you gonna live? Gimme an address.'

I was startled but ready. Somewhere in my wallet I had the address Jimmy Rittenhaus had given me. I pulled it out and started hunting. My ten grand piled up on the counter as the wallet emptied: traveller's cheques, high-denomination notes and bills.

'Hold it!' I looked up. 'Hold it, hold it, hold it!' I looked around at the line. People were nodding and smiling. My inquisitor was smiling too. 'What the hell's all this?'

'It's in here somewhere, officer, honestly.'

'This money?'

'Oh, that? Just some money I brought with me.'

'Why didnya say so?' And I was welcomed aboard. I collected my bags from the revolving console and got outside without the aid of a skycap. The afternoon weather was blowy and blue, bright on my stretched-out senses. New York! I took a good first look.

A line of yellow cabs waited along the curb some way to my left. I started towards them.

I hadn't got far before someone else was yelling, 'Hold it!' The driver of the first cab waved me away urgently, as if I was carrying typhoid and not luggage. I put it down and looked around. Quite far in the opposite direction a huge black man was waving me over. His bald head shone like a beacon.

'What the fuck does he want?' I asked the agitated driver. His hands flapped at me desperately. I caught the word 'despatcher'.

'Ya gotta go through the despatcher, bud. Get outa here . . .'

I peered down the line. All the cabmen looked back with the same message. Outa here! Behind the despatcher, I now noticed, half the world and its luggage surged restlessly. I moved over to join them.

The whoop of tyres almost threw me off my feet. 'Hey, man, wanna ride?'

Both doors hung out at me. A black face hanging away from the wheel, white teeth, red T-shirt, one arm stretched across like a flying catch. 'Man, man, move it, move it! Gimme them bags!'

I hurled them in front thinking only to dive in the back after them. He hooked them under his arm as we took off, screaming back at the despatcher, 'Fuck you!' Doors still open, I hung on to the back of the front seats until my man started steering. 'Whooee!'

'Bloody hell . . .' I croaked.

'You British?'

'Yes, I am.'

'All *right*!'

'Are you a cab?'

'Am I a cab? Man, am I a cab? I am a man, brother, an' don't you forget it!'

'Yes, yes, absolutely.'

'I am a man, in a car, with some British guy who might just be a total asshole. Man, you is completely in my powah, you know what I'm sayin?'

'I think so, yes.' I settled back, ready for I knew not what.

'You got cab fare?'

'Sure I have.'

'Where to?'

'Er . . .' I still hadn't found Jimmy's address.

'That's it, man, know what I mean? I ax you where to, you don' know. You be jes like ev'ybody else, know what I'm sayin'? You ain't got no direction. Your *life* ain't got no direction.'

'I'll find it in a minute.' I started hunting again in the wallet, this time more furtively. My friend just shook his head.

'Man, man. I'll jes head for the city, I guess.'

We climbed onto the expressway. Green signs, blue shields, unfamiliar destinations: Lincoln Parkway, Queens.

Backs of cars across four lanes ahead came up ever faster as we flew. I could see the red speedometer line run by the numbers from where I sat: 70, 80, 90. The expressway was full of holes. We had no suspension. We ricocheted from impact to impact. I tried to keep below the parapet of seats where the ten grand could stay out of range of the driver's mirror. I gripped the howling driveshaft with my knees. Every so often the roof came down and beat me on the head.

'Man, whatchoo playin' at down there?'

'I'm fine, honestly.'

'Regulations say sit well back in your seat.' As if to emphasise the importance of safety and comfort he dredged a massive ghetto-blaster from the floor near his feet and switched it on. The shattered atmosphere filled with funk.

Fumbling with the wallet now trapped beneath my thigh, I watched the landscape flashing past. Sunny towers sprouted all around, none of them Manhattan Skyline. I didn't like to ask. My pilot's bare brown arms stuck through the wheel, long hands beating a hard tattoo on top of the dash. Round his bony wrists I noticed beaded bracelets, red, white, blue and black. He took something from the ashtray, stuck it in his mouth, lit it from a zippo while the car drove itself. An aromatic haze clouded the chaos. Just in time my hand closed over the scrap of paper. I leaned forward. 'I say . . .'

'Wanna hit, brother?'

'I say I've found the address. Where we're going.'

'You ain't goin' nowhere man. I can tell. Have a hit.'

'Oh, OK.' How much more paranoid could I get?

Wooster is a street off Broadway, in SoHo. One of Jimmy's many pads was a loft on Wooster, near the corner of Broome, between Grand and Spring. What seemed like seconds later I was there. We went over a bridge. I saw the skyline. 'It's heavier at night,' I was told. We drove downtown from uptown, passed through Chelsea, the Village. This was real New York. The traffic slowed and stopped. Horns played. New Yorkers crowded the sidewalks, the delis, the smart joints and the tyre marts. The cross-streets were like ballet: slow, stop. Slow, stop. The sidelit traffic oozed to the rhythm of the lights. Yellow cabs pulled across impossible openings to pick up fares.

'There's a God at every cross-street in New York,' my friend told me.

'Is there?'

'If you're an African.'

In the quiet street, dark below warehouses, he gave me his card, looked me in the eye. I glanced down,

DOCTOR LOVE
Parapsychologist of Soul

and the address of a roller-rink in Brooklyn.

'You git down there, man, any night, if you got the balls. Get away from all this tourist honky shit. Jes ax for me, OK?'

'How about tonight? Could you pick me up?' I had parted with the kind of tip people give who are thankful to be alive.

'Man, you get you own ass down to *me*. I don't drive no Gypsy Cab at night. The night is right for action. Kinda action make a white ass honky like you shit with fear. Think you can handle that?'

'I think so.'

'I don't think so. Remember. The gates of Heaven don't open till eleven.'

As the battered cab sashayed away through the garbage and street steam I noticed the doctor's back bumper-sticker: PARADOXICAL GENETIC INFUSION.

'Ten grand. That's all that's left.'

'That's not much. Christ!' To Jimmy Rittenhaus it was not. His mother had left him a bank at a conveniently early age. Over the years he had hardly changed. The worry lines which cash crises cause were absent from his bland, shifty face.

His loft was three storeys up, the whole floor of an old warehouse. High-tech decor, waterbeds and scaffold walls. Jimmy and I lounged on hessian bean-bags.

'You lost *everything*?' He seemed impressed.

'Everything. Except this ten spot.'

'Jesus! What about Natasha and the kids?'

'They're OK at the moment. Living with her mother.'

'They don't mind you bailing out?'

'I'm not bailing out. I'm here to make money. That's what America's all about, isn't it?'

We mused on this while Jimmy rolled a joint. His monkey, Oedipus Rex, hung by one long arm, watching. Jimmy shook his head. 'These yanks . . .'

'Shouldn't be too difficult, should it?'

The warehouse windows framed violet light like paintings. Jimmy sighed. 'Ten grand. It's not much of a grub stake.'

'I just thought, anything's possible over here.'

Jimmy yawned. 'I expect you're right.'

The bistro on the corner of Mercer smelled of fresh-baked corn-bread and apples. The menu stood on an easel in the open doorway. Scrub-faced waitresses wore striped aprons over their jeans. One of them brought us a candle and a carafe of wine. 'Hi.'

We ate boeuf stroganoff and crêpes. I leaned back in my bentwood chair, pleased with America.

'It's funny you should live on a street called Wooster.'

'Yeah? Why?'

'You know. Bertie and Jeeves and all that.'

'Oh. Yeah.'

'I love Bertie and Jeeves, don't you?'

'Not much.'

We were ready for Brooklyn when Jimmy remembered his new video camera. 'Of course we need to video it, if it's any good. I video everything these days.'

Something I remembered Doctor Love saying made me cautious. 'Honestly, Jimmy. I don't know if it's the kind of place you want to go with a lot of expensive equipment.'

'You don't know this town like I do.'

I waited on the sidewalk. Jimmy reappeared minutes later, state-of-the-art from head to toe.

As it turned out it wasn't the kind of place yellow cabs wanted to go, either. In spite of losing everything back home, the ten grand made me feel rich. 'I'll double anything on the clock,' I told the fifth hack.

'Triple.'

'OK.'

'Hop in, bub.'

Dwarfed by the skyline we howled over Brooklyn Bridge. On Flatbush we picked up two outriders. They had red helmets, white T-shirts, bare black arms, twisting the grips of their fat-wheeled monsters. One drove between us and the kerb, teeth bared white through the closed windows of the cab. When we slowed for a red light they speeded up. They wheelied away with a noise like Bofors guns.

We saw the bikes again a few minutes later. They were propped against the wall outside the Galaxie Rollerdrome. I paid off the cab. He hardly checked his change before hanging a fast U and shuddering off at speed.

Sounds similar to those of the Doctor's ghetto-blaster blew out through the narrow door. Just inside, a turnstile with tickets two bucks apiece. I peeled off a five and handed it to a loose-limbed giant in a red baseball cap. His outsize adam's apple jerked with a laconic, 'Skate-rental, right over there . . .' handing back a faded bill.

But we were rooted to the spot. Even a playboy as jaded as Jimmy had never seen anything like this. A million sparks of fractured light from the giant mirrorball flickered over the astonishing scene. Pounding music almost drowned the sustained roar of a thousand roller-wheels on maple. Whistles blew.

Skate-rental or no skate-rental the idea of joining the rhythmic serpent of humanity on the rink seemed ill advised. They flowed effortlessly around, turning, weaving, diving through each other's legs. Hundreds of bodies rolling together gave a

— 13 —

deceptive sense of languor to the fact that the whole mass was moving at thirty miles an hour at least. I had never rollerskated. I looked at Jimmy. Neither had he.

We sidled over to the refreshment counter and bought drinks. We leaned against the bar and tried our best to look loose. One problem with sitting out was the attention it drew to the fact that we were the only white folks in the place. I could see no sign of Doctor Love. Jimmy said, quite loudly, 'This is revolutionary! These people aren't just skating. They're bloody dancing on wheels!'

I said, 'Absolutely,' as unobtrusively as I could. Jimmy started rigging up his equipment with feverish fingers. It all folded out of black leather cases and became alarmingly noticeable. He wore a power-pak on his back. In one hand he held his top-of-the-line camera. In the other, high over his head, I was dismayed to see a high-powered lamp.

'Is that thing essential?' I said, arms full of empty cases.

'Of course,' he retorted, adding something about colour definition that I didn't catch. I hoped no one else did either.

Jimmy loped away on his two-hundred-dollar sneakers, his ferret face pointing relentlessly. He had moved the peak of his Dodgers cap around to the back of his sloping head. He went to the edge of the rink and faced the oncoming skaters, nursing his camera to his nose. He raised the lamp.

The pile-up when he switched on was spectacular. Blinded by the light, the casualties just kept on coming. Jimmy kept on filming, apparently unmoved. When the bodies were about ten deep he wandered off.

A slinky girl with glossy hair and lips and short striped shorts was practising spins on her own over by the skate-rental. She had obviously caught Jimmy's eye and distracted him from the main event. He headed for her with tireless determination. She looked up briefly when the lamp went on, then carried on. She was indifferent to Jimmy but her spins got zippier. Jimmy flexed his knees as the camera rolled.

When the skateguards arrived, Jimmy at first didn't notice.

There were four of them. They wore Tonton Macoutes shades and silver whistles round their necks. One of them blew his in Jimmy's ear.

'Hey!' Jimmy yelped in outrage and abandoned the shot. They stood around him impassively, arms folded, their skate-wheels moving imperceptibly back and forward.

I couldn't hear their voices. Nor could I read their lips. The slinky girl continued practising as the guards formed tightly around Jimmy and moved off. Jimmy waved his equipment feebly. The peak of his baseball cap had shifted over one ear.

The fallen skaters were still sorting themselves out. It was now possible to see through to the area in the centre of the rink. This had been decked out as an oasis. Plastic palm trees leaned over yellow plastic chairs. Taking it easy in these were the local élite. I recognised the T-shirts of the two fat-wheel bikers.

One stood out from the rest. Even sitting down he was tall. He was majestic. He wore a turban of glowing gold cloth. A black pencil of hair framed his lips. In one drooping jewelled hand hung a joint the size of a Dead Sea Scroll. His hooded eyes lowered as he inspected Jimmy. The bikers and the skateguards and the rest of the cabal looked on.

It was an absorbing spectacle and I was giving it my full attention when a voice behind me said, 'Hey, Honky.'

I writhed around. 'Me?'

'Yeah, mo'fucker. You.' It was another skateguard. 'You with him?' He indicated Jimmy with a nod. It seemed futile to deny it.

Oh, to be tall and black! As I crossed the rink with my captor the Red Sea parted but not in friendship. Curious, hostile eyes looked down on me. I felt white and short and thoroughly unwholesome.

The Leader's eyes were yellow slits, like a cat. He drew long and deep on the doobie. In the smoke the lisping voice was the last thing to be expelled, 'Mo'fu'sss' was all his lungs could handle. All around him nodded sagely.

One of the bikers, a bullet-headed seven-footer built like the Michelin man, was more verbal. 'What you think happen some honkyass mo'fuckers come down here fuck up our rink? Fuckin' uptown honkies?'

It didn't take an outsize imagination to guess. My mind spurred on by terror, my hand fumbled in my pocket and came up with Doctor Love's card. I held it out to the Leader as if it were frankincense and myrrh. He took it slowly and studied it for a long time. His eyes opened slightly as he looked at me. 'How you know Love?'

'I met him. He said I should come down here.' My head rotated like a cornered turtle. 'He's not around, is he?'

The card had brought a moment's respite. It was all Jimmy needed. 'We're making a movie, you see.'

They all looked at Jimmy. The Leader eyed him narrowly. The bulbous biker, probably the Court Executioner, said, 'That ain't no movie camera.'

But Jimmy was off and running. When it came down to technicalities he was hard to suppress. He spoke freely and at length of pre-production and storyboards, and the vital importance of videotape in research and development of movies. The name of Steven Spielberg came into it twice.

'This a *Hollywood* Movie you talkin' bout?' The Leader was more lucid now. His fingertips stroked delicately along a dusty plastic palm-frond. Jimmy raised his equipment assertively.

'Certainly Hollywood.'

And I said, 'Absolutely!'

Back on the street we were jaunty. We had been ushered from the Galaxie with considerable ceremony. The Leader parted from us only reluctantly, with wringing hands and promises to meet again at an early date. Jimmy gave the name and address of his production company, somewhere uptown. 'It's just the New York office.'

'I didn't know anything about that,' I said.

'Neither did I,' spluttered Jimmy as we hurried away, 'until just now.'

— 16 —

There weren't any cabs but we found one. We had charmed lives.

It was a perfect New York morning, still and blue. The sounds of the Great City floated in through our open windows. We had woken late and were lounging, considering brunch at a joint on Greene. Steamed eggs and French toast. We sipped cappuccinos from a new Italian gadget Jimmy was anxious to demonstrate. His weasel face creased into a smile. 'They were pretty fucking street-wise, those guys.'

'God, yes,' nodding in the fragrant steam. 'We sure fooled 'em.'

'Hey! British!' floated up from the street below. Directly below. I looked at Jimmy, askance. His smile faded. We had forgotten about Doctor Love.

When I stuck my head out he executed a high leap on his denim skating boots. He was not the only skater in the street. The Leader and his immediate circle, about a dozen of them, were strung out down the middle of it, dancing in formation.

Along the sidewalks a crowd was gathering. Traffic was building up. Doctor Love swooped down the line of spectators with his hat. His white teeth blazed as he held it up to me. 'Next stop Hollywood!'

'How are we going to get out of this?' It was many hours later before Jimmy and I were alone again, in the littered loft.

'Maybe you shouldn't get out of it.' Jimmy looked inscrutable. 'You want to make a fortune. Maybe there really is a movie in these guys.'

'I don't know the first thing about making movies.'

'There's a friend of ours who does.'

'Who?'

'Henry Pelham. He's living out there now.'

'But would he want to?'

'He'll certainly listen to me. He's living in my beach house.'

I bought the tickets for Jimmy and me to fly the Redeye to the Coast. After all, I was the producer. They came to five hundred dollars. I managed to keep the number of my stars down to ten, but even so, flight for them was impossibly over budget. Doctor Love, who knew about cars, found the solution. It was a Pontiac Stratocruiser. With new tyres and autotune it came to two thousand bucks. An investment, we all agreed. We could sell it again in LA when we got a deal. Privately I hoped not. It was beautiful. I'd never seen a car so big. The skaters left before us on their trek, happy packed-in faces waving goodbye for ever to Brooklyn.

Jimmy gave them the Malibu address and I gave them some expenses. We would see them there.

'They won't not show up, will they?' A moment's fear for my investment.

'Not a hope,' said Jimmy.

We left after a celebration dinner at an Afghani joint on Second Avenue. Six hours of inflight cocktails later it was still time for dinner in LA. Henry, Viscount Pelham, was waiting for us at the barrier, lantern jaw hanging open in welcome. He wore a white suit, an OE tie, and a suntan.

'Welcome to the colonies,' he said.

His Eldorado was parked on the white zone with the top down. Gold coronets were monogrammed on the doors. The numberplate read 4TUNE.

We got on the San Diego Freeway. I sat behind with my head tilted back, looking up at the stars. Wind rushed in my ears as we cruised through the warm velour night.

We came off the freeway at a street called Sunset. Henry said, 'We're going into town. There's a party.'

Outside Le Dome the matching stretches lined the kerb. I had never seen stretched limousines. Henry dismissed them with a gesture, as the valet whisked the Eldorado away. 'That's what this town's all about. You'll get used to it.'

At the palm-and-glass entrance, admission was blocked by a sign: PRIVATE PARTY. Henry stooped to whisper in a flunky's ear.

'Good evening Lord Pelham.' The man stood aside smiling. 'Two extra guests? Of course, your Lordship.'

Inside, the Californians crowded between green walls and pink-lit alcoves: dark men in blazers and open-neck shirts, spangle-bangle women of uncertain age with blonde manes and sun-dried cleavages.

As we pushed to the bar Henry hissed, 'It's Gregory Peck's birthday.'

'Oh.' I looked around.

Henry ordered drinks. They came with a tab. 'What's this?'

'That's a no-host bar this evening, gents.' The bartender's perfect teeth shone with condescension.

'Shit.' Henry pulled a credit card from a Gucci folder. He slapped it down. It read *Rt Hon. The Lord Henry Pelham.*

In partnership with Henry my fortune in the movies seemed assured. I went down to the luxuriously appointed mensroom. A total stranger gave me a line of coke. 'Hi!' It seemed a good word for it.

I woke in the morning and couldn't remember the drive home. I lay in a room full of sunlight filtered through bamboo. The ocean sucked and boomed a restful thunder. Nothing is urgent, it seemed to say.

I opened the french windows and walked out straight onto hot crunchy sand. I breathed in deep and looked around. The sun felt hot on my face and chest. It blazed on the breakers where they curled like glass, just before they crashed. Beyond the surf line a group of pelicans bobbed about on the sluggish swell. In a house built on stilts in Malibu I felt a long way from London.

An old man jogged by. He was naked. He bent forward forty-five degrees, getting momentum from his own gravity. His penis flapped against his scrawny leg, flap, flap, flap. He raised a withered hand. 'Hi!'

A girl with a ponytail trotted past on horseback. I raised my arm in greeting. 'Hi!' But she didn't respond.

Wooden steps led up to the deck and the rest of the beach-house. Henry appeared at the top of them. 'Shaw, you bugger. Feeling rough?' He wore turquoise Bermuda shorts with white seahorses. He held up a jug of red liquid. 'Hair of the dog . . .?'

The wooden house and deck were hidden under bougain-villea, purple, red and green. We sat on white chairs. Henry had lent me a straw hat. We raised our Bloody Marys to each other.

'A Paradise, Henry.' I sipped contentedly.

'Tell the landlord.' Henry nodded at Jimmy.

Jimmy said, 'Go on, Paul, pitch.'

'Jimmy says you've got an idea for a movie.' Suddenly it was two against one. 'In this town,' Henry continued blandly, 'you have to learn to pitch. Preferably in one line.'

'Well, er . . .'

'What's the story? What's it about?'

'Well, you know, it's not so much a story as a . . .'

'Visual experience,' said Jimmy.

'That's it! Absolutely! A visual experience.'

'Ha!' Henry leaned back and tilted his hat. 'Just try selling *that* to a studio.'

'We've got a video, haven't we, Jimmy?'

'Look,' Henry said, beating the table with the blade of his hand, 'in Hollywood you have to have a story. Beginning, middle and end. Right?'

'It's about rollerskating,' I said, hopefully.

'And black religious culture,' Jimmy added. 'Paradoxical Genetic Infusion.'

Henry groaned, 'Christ!'

*

'Look, whatever you do, when this guy arrives, no genetic infusions, right?'

'Right.'

'Movie moguls don't use words like paradoxical.'

'Right.'

'And no religious culture. Particularly black. Stick to the story we worked out.'

It was two days later. We had come up with a story, an outline. We had kicked it around. It had a beginning, a middle and a variety of endings. The final choice of end would depend on whether the movie was to be comedy or drama. We were keeping our options open. It had a hero and a heroine, neither of them specifically black. We were keeping our options open there, too. The rollerskating had become optional.

'Nothing set in stone at this stage,' Henry advised. I couldn't help worrying about my stars. There wasn't much left of the movie we had kicked around in Jimmy's loft.

I said, 'I think the skating's absolutely the key element. Don't you, Henry?'

Henry said, 'The main thing at this stage is to get a deal. That's all that counts. It's called the Donald Duck syndrome.'

'What's that?'

'Supposing this guy today, who's got a really strong position at Paramount, says he wants Donald Duck to direct it, or write it, or star in it, or whatever the fuck, we say "Great!", right? That's the Donald Duck syndrome.'

In my official capacity as producer I had laid on a lavish lunch built round the known or rumoured tastes of our mogul. Henry was able to recommend the ideal caterer.

Roger (pronounced Rojay) was 'big in the Colony'. I didn't like him. I didn't like his prices, either. He had invented 'cuisine Californienne'. Derived from nouvelle cuisine, it adhered religiously to the principal of 'less is more'.

'You can't be serious!' I said, gaping at a photo of a single crayfish garnished with three zucchini flowers.

'Mistair Graumann just loves crayfish,' lisped Rojay. 'He's a real gourmet.'

'More than one, though, surely?'

'You obviously don't understand *cuisine Californienne*,' Rojay said, whisking the photo away.

'I don't understand how a thing like that can be sixty dollars.'

'These dishes are *design*!' Rojay ran his fingers through his tight black curls. His chubby cheeks flushed pink. 'If you don't like you can . . . fick off!'

'It's all right, Rojay.' Henry tilted back, pushing his hat up off his brow. 'Now. What about the wine?'

Rojay's face cleared. He glanced at me contemptuously, then back at Henry. 'Mistair Graumann adores '54 La Tache, Lord Henry.'

'At lunch?' Even Henry looked surprised. 'With fish?'

'How much is it?' I said. I didn't know much about wine, but I had my suspicions.

'Expensive,' Henry said, grimly.

'Five or six hundred,' Rojay said with a malicious flourish.

'Don't you just love Rojay's food, Kenny?' Henry nibbled and sipped before he spoke. We were seated under a specially erected marquee on the deck. Flowers arranged by Rojay's friend Martin abounded. Two curly-headed young waiters hovered. Rojay attended to the wine.

'I hate it.' Kenny Graumann wore a bright blue sportcoat over his open Lacoste shirt. Round glasses with gold rims kept his expression inscrutable. Rojay snickered and poured Kenny another glassful. Fifty bucks worth, I calculated.

'But I had a triple bypass, see?' Kenny sipped and licked his purple lips. 'No more chicken-fried steaks for me.'

'All those movies take their toll, I suppose.' His Lordship sipped carefully at his own glass.

Jimmy gazed out to sea, obviously uninterested in Kenny Graumann.

'Thinkin' a packin' it in,' Kenny growled. 'I made my dough arready. What the hell.'

'Life in the old dog yet, I should say.' Henry with hard heartiness patted Kenny on the coat.

'That's what my wife says.' Kenny looked a little rueful. Rojay snickered knowingly. Kenny looked at him. 'You can never be too thin or too rich. That's her philosophy.'

'You'll just have to keep on working,' said Henry.

'And dieting,' said Rojay.

'And dieting,' said Kenny, shaking his head. He took a lengthy pull at '54 La Tache.

After the kiwi-fruit and fresh raspberry torte, Rojay filled three balloon glasses with 'something very *spacial*'. It was five-star cognac brewed in 1936. I took a good swig of mine to deaden the pain of mental arithmetic. As Kenny Graumann said, what the hell.

'So how about it, Kenny?' Henry shifted in his chair in a flexing sort of way.

Kenny lit a large cigar. 'OK. You're right. I've had my lunch – there's no such thing as a free lunch in this town. So go ahead and pitch.'

Henry nodded at me. I had another go at the '36. It tasted like metal polish. 'Well, you see, in the story, there's this chap. This guy. He's from Brooklyn . . .'

'Not unlike *Saturday Night Fever* . . .' Henry nodded encouragingly.

'No,' I continued, 'not unlike *Saturday Night Fever*. Anyway, as I say, there's this guy . . .'

'What kinda guy?' Kenny took out his cigar and inspected the chewed end.

'What kind?' I said.

'He's a . . . well . . .' Henry spread his arms deprecatingly, '. . . he's a good-looking guy.'

'Yes, yes,' I said.

'OK, so he's good-looking. Good.' Kenny, apparently satisfied, examined his blue leather cigar-case minutely.

'Absolutely,' I went on, warming to my theme. 'Anyway, in this story, you see, it's the girl who's – '

'Girl? What girl?' Kenny was looking carefully up one of the tubes.

'The girl in the story. She's – '

'She's the female lead, Kenny.' Henry explained patiently.

'Yes, yes,' I said, 'only in this movie it's the girl who's a really good, er . . .'

'Dancer,' said Henry. 'She's a really good dancer.' Rojay snickered.

'OK, OK.' Kenny nodded with dawning comprehension. He had tipped the contents of his cigar-case onto the table before him. I was surprised and not a little thrown to observe among the first class Havana Corona Coronas six bright brass objects with lead tips. For the first time Jimmy took an interest in the conversation.

'Aren't those dum-dums for a '48 Magnum?'

'You gotta be kiddin'.' Kenny became animated for the first time. 'These is fer a Colt '45.'

'Really?' said Jimmy. 'Have you got one?'

'Have I got one?' said Kenny, really warming up. 'You better believe it!' He reached down under his chair for the pigskin briefcase he had placed there at the beginning of the meal. He hoisted it onto the table and undid two gold locks. Lifting the lid to obscure our view of the interior, he rummaged for a moment. When the lid went down he was gun in hand.

'Solid silver, pearl handles, the woiks. Here – ' he handed the gun to Jimmy – 'take a look.'

Jimmy examined the gun. 'But why do you keep the bullets in your cigar-case?'

'Gun-laws, that's why!' said Kenny in disgust. 'Not allowed to carry a loaded gun. This is the nearest I can get.'

'Why should you want to?' Henry was fighting his irritation. 'Carry a gun, I mean?'

Kenny spun the magazine in a businesslike way. 'There's a helluva lotta schwartzers in this town.'

'All *right*!'

'*Oooeee!*'

I had opened my mouth to continue pitching. It remained open.

'This is the *place*!'

'*Malibu*!'

'*Hollywood*! '

My companions twisted in their seats, Kenny in particular, as the wooden deck came alive to the rumble of forty roller-wheels.

They had dressed for the occasion. The Leader was a striking sight. From turban-top to wheels he measured a good eight feet. I saw Kenny furtively slipping shells into chambers. Jimmy and I were fervently embraced. Henry and Kenny were introduced. Rojay introduced himself: 'Hi, I am Rojay. I am delightful.' He shook hands with every single one.

Kenny relaxed after a while. He slipped the Colt into his pocket. Jimmy said to him, 'These guys are in the movie.'

'Oh, yeah?'

Henry looked at Jimmy, passing a finger across his throat. Doctor Love spun by. 'Man, we IS the movie!'

Kenny looked at me with his hard, colourless eyes. 'Is this movie about rollerskating?'

I thought, what the hell. 'Yes.'

He waggled his cigar impatiently. 'Why the hell didnya say so?'

Henry rallied fast. 'You didn't give us a chance.'

'When I wuz a kid I wuz a skater. Good, clean, American fun.'

'Yes,' said Henry, 'that's what we thought.'

At this moment the Leader, overwhelmed by the sight of ocean, tore off his skates and clothes and ran into the waves. The others followed, including Rojay. 'Hold on,' he screamed, 'I am coming!'

By evening we were back to three, surprised and pleased. The marquee and the waiters were gone. The skaters had

squeezed Rojay into the Stratocruiser, next to the Leader. He
had undertaken to guide them to the Tropicana Motel.

'You'll adore it,' he squealed. 'It's in Boystown.'

Kenny Graumann swirled off down the dusty beach road
in his Corniche. Before he left he said, 'I think I got just the
guy for this picture. A real star.'

Jimmy stretched and yawned. 'Looks as though you've got
it made,' he said. Thinking of ten tabs at the Tropicana, I said,
'I certainly hope so.'

A few days later, Kenny called. He wanted us to rent a big
rink and throw a skating party. 'He says its the best way of
pitching to this guy,' Henry said blandly. 'I agree.'

'Who is this guy, though?'

'He won't say, obviously. A very big star.'

I shook my head. 'I don't know.'

'Once you've attached your star you can write your own
ticket.'

'Isn't there a simpler way?'

'Kenny says not. We'd better call Rojay.'

'Oh, God, not Rojay!'

'Can you think of anyone better?'

We called Rojay. He was thrilled. He knew just the place: a
rink in the San Fernando Valley. Jack Nicholson skated there
all the time. Rojay could guarantee lots of stars at the party.
It would only cost five grand.

I stared at Henry in horror.

'Five grand isn't much.'

'It's all I've got left!'

Henry shrugged. 'It's your movie. You can quit any time
you like.'

Two weeks of unbroken sunshine later the big day arrived.
Dusk was falling as we drove through Malibu Canyon to the

Ventura Freeway. We got off at Burbank, home of Donald Duck.

The rink was gay with flowers. It was larger than the Galaxie, emptier, like an aircraft hangar. Sounds echoed hollowly. Rojay's waiters passed among the scant throng with laden trays. They wore rollerskates and shorts.

There was no sign of Jack Nicholson. My own stars were there in strength, dressed for success. They greeted me like a hero. Doctor Love skated over and slapped my hand. He was wearing a new denim outfit including denim skating boots. He made me feel more hopeful. I took a glass of something from a passing tray.

Together we ambled over to the buffet. Various examples of *cuisine Californienne* were on display.

'Man, I'm glad I isn't hungry!' declared Doctor Love.

'You should be glad you're not paying for it,' I said, with feeling.

'I heard that.'

I sipped my sweet, cloying, Californian champagne. 'That's a pretty cool outfit, Love . . .'

'Didn' pay for that either. Doctor Love pulled the peak of his familiar cap over one eye and winked with the other. 'Why do you think they call me Doctor Love?'

Party people were beginning to filter into the gaps between waiters. They were the same as those at Le Dome. A buzz by the door caused heads to turn.

There is something about stars, about the atmosphere surrounding them. It is caused as much by others as by themselves, a sense of distance, of untouchability, as if they were lepers.

This one entered with Kenny Graumann and a woman in a big fur coat. I couldn't place him but I knew he was a star. He was small and old and wore a cap like Doctor Love.

People started sipping self-consciously and shooting sideways glances.

'It's . . .'

'Who?' I asked a passer-by.

'Victor Ventura.'

'Ah,' I recalled some swashbuckling epics from my youth. Henry skated up, hanging onto things. He hung on to me. His breath was hot and sweet.

'Great party!'

'Absolutely!'

'Not skating?'

'Maybe later.'

'You see he's here?'

'That's him, is it?'

'Of course.'

'Bit old, isn't he?'

'Ssshh. Go over and talk to him. Go on.'

I tacked around in his vicinity, like a lot of other people. He was sitting in a booth, alone with the woman. There was no sign of Kenny.

'Mister Ventura . . .?'

He looked up. 'Hello?' Under the cap the bronze hair glowed suspiciously.

'I'm Paul Shaw.'

'Oh, yes?'

'It's my party, you know.'

He nodded and smiled. 'Very nice.'

The woman smiled, too. 'Sweet of you to invite us.' She had removed the coat. She was unglamorous, with grey hair and a flowered frock. Her motherly air appealed to me. 'Do you mind if I sit down?'

'Of course,' she moved up, protecting him from sitting next to me.

I leaned across her. 'So what d'you think about the movie, Mr Ventura?'

'Huh?' His blue eyes were cloudy.

'The rollerskating . . .'

'Oh, sure, sure . . .'

'Mr Ventura loves rollerskating,' his companion smiled with kindly eyes.

'I love it.' Victor Ventura nodded and showed his perfect teeth. His fleshy face under the cap was purplish blue.

'Hey Vic! Get ya skates on!' Kenny Graumann rolled up and crashed into the table. 'Come on, wassermadderwiya?' And they all disappeared.

I wandered rinkside and watched. The Leader and his team were staging their display of skate-dancing. It was hard to say if anyone was aware of it. Doctor Love was operating solo. I saw that someone was aware of *him*: a girl in a rinkside banquette followed his every move. She was young, around seventeen, bulging slightly in her tight candy-stripe sweater and spandex pants. Dark hair framed her freckled face. On one wrist she wore a tiny gold watch with a thin black strap.

Around the edge the landlubbers, Jimmy and Henry included, struggled experimentally, remaining within safe clinging distance of the rail. Inside, a more confident stream of skaters glided by. This stratum was shortly joined by Victor Ventura and his lady. They moved in slow waltz time. Under the jaunty cap Victor faced squarely into his partner's matronly bosom.

'Don't he skate beautiful?' I looked up to find Kenny Graumann at my side, his face rapt with admiration.

'A little slow, perhaps?' I demurred as diplomatically as I could. Kenny gripped his chest with outraged pride. 'So he's got a heart condition. Whaddya wanna do, kill the guy?'

Sitting around the Tropicana pool I broke the solemn news.

'His doctor said no. He's looking for more sedentary roles.'

'Man, thass OK. We din wan that ol' honky in our movie anyways.' My stars lounged on the astroturf, glowing in their bright briefs.

'But that's just it, don't you see. I don't think there's going to be any movie. Without a star I can't get a deal.'

'No sweat, British. We cin wait.'

I had made my way to the Tropicana with some difficulty by bus. I tried to explain. 'Look, guys. I'm broke.'

'Broke? You can't be broke! Man, you're rich!'

'I'm not rich. I'm very poor.'

'You hang with rich folks. You must be rich.'

'I used to be rich. The people I know are rich. My business in England went bust. I came over here to make a fortune with my last ten grand. Now I don't know what I'm going to do.'

'Go home, brother. Go home.'

'I can't go home. I'm a bankrupt. I can't get work. My wife and kids are living with her mother, waiting for me to save the day. I just can't face . . .' I shook my head, facing it all for the first time.

Doctor Love came over and sat down. 'Relax, British, relax. We all be OK, don't you worry 'bout us.'

'Will you really? I feel so awful. What will you all do?'

One of the bikers spotted the silver lining. 'We still got the car. We go home, I guess . . .'

'What about the bill here, though . . .' I stared around. 'Oh, God . . .'

'Thass OK. We'll go at night.' They started laughing and hitting the ground.

One of them passed me a bottle of Mountain Dew. 'What you need is a drink.' I took a swig and felt a little better.

Doctor Love put his arm round my shoulder. 'British, what you need is a job.'

I took another swig. 'What kind of job? I can't do anything.'

'You cin talk.'

'Yeah, British. You sure talk nice.'

I shook my head.

'Educated white boy like you should be in charge of something.'

'Yes, yes,' I nodded. The wine was coursing nicely through my veins. 'But what?'

A red Mercedes sports car pulled into the parking lot.

Doctor Love said, 'Hey! Here comes my girlfriend.'

The rinkside girl walked over, smiling. 'Having a party?'

I said, 'More of a wake, really.'

Doctor Love said, 'My man here lookin' for a job. Fine upstandin' Britisher like him outa be in charge of something.'

The girl sat down. 'Hi, I'm Tracey.' Her voice lilted up at the end of each word. She held out her hand to me. 'You can be in charge of our house.'

I stared at her.

'Sure. Mom just fired the butler.'

'The butler!' My voice sounded far away. My brain buzzed with wine. She lilted on. 'He turned out to be a transvestite. Mom found him in her room wearing one of her dresses.'

'All *right!*' The brothers could dig it.

'He tore the dress when he took it off, so she fired him.'

I tried to take it in. Doctor Love said, 'How much this job pay?'

'Around three thousand, I guess.'

'Three thousand a year?' I said, floundering.

Her throaty laugh rang round the dusty palm trees. 'A month.'

'Three thousand dollars a month!?' I yelped.

'Ooooeee!' said the brothers.

'Plus extras . . .'

'British, you got it made.'

Doctor Love could see I still needed pushing. 'What can you lose?'

I liked at Tracey. She was smiling encouragement. 'I'll score a lot of Brownie points, finding a guy like you.'

'Well, I suppose . . .'

'Come and look at the house, anyways.'

I rose to my feet amid general applause. 'What the hell.'

— 2 —

We hung a right onto Santa Monica Boulevard and went right again. A sign said BEVERLY HILLS. Something tightened around my heart. I tried to relax by chattering to Tracey. 'This is a great car.' It was bright and fast and smelt expensive.

'Really,' she said.

I felt I should be wearing a bowler hat. Trying not to sound too fatherly, I said, 'What do you do, Tracey?'

'School.' Her bare legs tramped the pedals.

'Oh.'

'Beverly Hills High.'

'That must be nice.'

'Shitty. Full of rich kids.'

A left on Sunset, then a right at the Beverly Hills Hotel. The houses here were half-hidden among shady trees. Gardeners stooped on manicured slopes. A few lefts and rights later we pulled up before gates. Winged griffons stood on stone pillars. The studded black blank between them looked like six-inch steel. Perched beside one of the griffons a cyclops scanned us. It made a faint whirring noise as it swept through its remorseless arc.

Tracey took a gadget out and pushed a button. The gate slowly swung open. I thought, 'Childe Rolande to the Dark Tower came.' A woolly mammoth of the pre-palaeolithic age stared at us from a bush. 'What is that?' I asked Tracey.

'Mom wanted a zoo, you know, like Chessingtown. When she married this guy she got one.'

'They're statues?'

'Sure.' Tracey scanned me with her incurious eyes. 'If they were living, they'd escape.'

Up the long drive I caught sight of other beasts, giraffes, sabre-toothed tigers, browsing among tennis courts and ornamental grottoes.

Passing through a tall screen of eucalyptus the house was suddenly revealed. Once I'd gone on a school outing to Framlingham Castle, Suffolk. It was built in the reign of King John, just before Magna Carta. Here it was again.

'You should feel at home here.' Tracey scrunched the car to a halt on the glistening gravel.

'I don't know, I – '

'Being a British aristocrat an' all.'

'I'm not an aristocrat.'

'Doctor Love says you are. You sound like one.'

'All the same.'

'Wait till my mom hears that accent.'

We parked by a circle of perfect grass. In the centre a flagpole, from which four flags flew. The top three I recognised: the Confederacy, the Stars and Stripes, the Californian Bear.

'What's that flag, the bottom one?' A 'K' fluttered in a laurel crown.

'Some dumb family crest.'

We walked across the drawbridge. Beneath us the moat was crystal clear. Artificial waves coursed by.

At the arched door Tracey tugged a bellpull. Musical chimes pealed within. I said, 'Don't you have a key?'

She looked at me incredulously. Behind an iron grille a trap flapped back. Framed in the aperture was a yellow, angular face.

'It's OK, Fong.' Tracey sounded conciliatory. 'It's only me.'

The slanted eyes slid suspiciously from side to side. 'Who this guy?'

'A friend.'

'Missee say no more boyflends.'

'He's not a boyfriend.' I shifted in huge unease. 'I've brought him to see Missee.'

'Missee no yin.'

'Let us in, Fong.'

'This guy no good.'

'This guy might be the new butler . . .'

'No likee butler!' And the trap snapped shut.

Tracey banged the studded door with her slim fist. 'Shit!'

I said, 'Oh, well . . .' I was about to add that perhaps the whole plan needed urgent revision, when another red sports car appeared and snarled up the drive. It was a Jaguar XK150.S.

Tracey's hand squeezed my elbow. She murmured, 'My mom . . .' and retreated a few steps across the drawbridge. 'Hi, Mom!'

Mom stepped out and teetered towards us on stacked, sling-back shoes. She had an hourglass figure no higher than five foot two. As she approached she pulled off a headscarf, revealing tight, auburn curls. Red lips slid back and embraced us both in a frozen smile. 'Well?'

'This is Paul.'

She looked into my face. Her eyes were black and bright.

I cleared my throat and held out my hand. 'How d'you do?'

Tracey said, 'Paul is British.'

Mom held out her hand just far enough for me to reach it. It was soft, warm, unresponsive. I could feel the cold bite of her rings.

'Hi.' She continued to search my face, only her eyes moving. I smiled weakly. At last she took her hand away and headed for the door. It stood open. The rest of Fong could now be seen. He was shorter than his mistress, in a white nylon jacket and black pants. He was smiling. Brown uneven teeth split his lemon face in a lopsided leer. Tracey's mom swept past him

— 34 —

without a glance. Tracey and I followed in her wake. Fong closed the door.

A staircase of the kind swept down by belles at balls swept up into the mist. A large portrait recognisable as Mom, dressed for just such an occasion, stood on an easel in the centre of the polished floor.

Tracey pulled at my limp hand before I could take more in. 'C'mon, quick, before she goes upstairs.'

I followed blindly along a labyrinth of striking decorative schemes. We came out in a large farmhouse kitchen. Tracey's mom stood by the open fridge, eating a piece of chicken. Fong sprang forward with iced tea.

'Napkin, Fong, napkin.'

'Ayee!' He disappeared into the next room, returning with a paper towel.

'Linen, goddammit, linen!'

'Solly, Missee . . .'

'Never mind.'

'I go find . . .'

'Forget it!'

'Solly, Missee.'

'Whaddya thinka my new hairdo, Fong?'

'Vey nice, Missee.'

She turned to me. 'You like it?'

'I said, 'Oh, ah . . .'

'Want some chicken?' She licked her fingers, dropping the bone and greasy napkin onto the scrubbed pine table. Fong leaped to scoop them up.

'No, thanks.'

'About all you get around here since David left.'

Fong shook his head, 'David vey bad boy . . .'

'He could cook.'

Tracey said, 'He was a fag.'

Her mom said, 'He was cute.'

'Paul knows a lot about cooking.' Tracey gave me a meaning look. 'Don't you.'

'Well, I . . .'

Her mom's black eyes bored into mine. 'Pity you're not available.'

'That's just it, Mom, you see . . .'

'You a domestic?' The eyes narrowed keenly.

'He's a British aristocrat, Mom!' Tracey leapt to my defence.

'He can speak for himself.'

I wished I could. 'The thing is, I, that is, Tracey here told me about, er, about the last chap . . .'

'He's never done it before but he might be interested. Mightn't you?'

I opened my mouth to speak, but words failed.

'OK.' Missee bustled from the room. I stared after her. Tracey said, 'Go on. Go for it.'

Back in the labyrinth I kept catching glimpses of her up ahead. Her heels tapped the same staccato rhythm on the varied floorings. When they stopped, and I couldn't see her any more, I felt myself seize up. My heart pounded in the hush. My shoulders and neck had stiffened painfully. My voice, when I called out, sounded strained and strange.

'Hallo?'

'Here,' came the reply. I followed the sound down a panelled passageway. A large heavy door with brass fittings stood before me. I knocked and entered.

The room I entered was not thirteenth-century. While not the aristocrat advertised by Tracey, I had hung about enough stately homes to recognise English Baroque.

Tracey's mom stood before an ornate marble fireplace between two huge Chinese urns. Although dwarfed she had no trouble holding her own.

'Siddown, honey.' She indicated a brocade armchair. I obeyed, tugging at my upper legs as I did so. I had dressed for the Tropicana. Now, I felt, my sweatshirt, sneakers and jeans were letting me down with a bump. I tried crossing my legs and thought better of it. I remembered seeing a TV interview once with King Hussein of Jordan. He had sat with spinx-like stillness, his hands resting regally along the arms off his chair. I had a shot at it, straightening my back.

'An aristocrat?'

I thought of Tracey and Doctor Love. I didn't want to let them down. 'Well . . .'

'To the manor born?'

'In a way.'

'But down on your luck?'

At last I could be honest. 'Yes.'

She sighed, 'Old money that just fades away.'

But something behind her distracted my attention. Over the fireplace there was an outsize painting in a gilt frame. The subject of the portrait was disturbingly familiar – that jacket, those gold-rimmed glasses. The thin mocking smile.

'What went wrong, in your case?'

'Oh, er, who's that in the portrait behind you, if you don't mind my asking?'

'That's my husband. What's that got to do with it?'

'You mean, your name is Mrs Kenny Graumann?'

'Sure, what of it?'

'I think you should ask him, that's all.'

'Ask him what? I don't get you.'

When I had told her my story, she said, 'He's not gonna hold that against you. A lotta people screw up in movies. He won't even remember. And it doesn't stop you being his butler, does it?'

'It might be a bit embarrassing, don't you think?'

'You can't embarrass my husband – he's got no feelings.'

'Oh.'

'Now my mother. Her you can embarrass.'

'Your mother?'

'She's coming to tea. Let's see you make with some old world service.'

'Today?'

'She'll be here at five. Get together with Fong and come up with something fancy.'

Sensing the interview was over, I started to rise.

'If you can handle it you're hired.'

I found my way back to the kitchen. There was no sign of Fong. There was no sign of anybody. A big wooden wall-clock ticked in the silence. Half-past four. The old neck and shoulder pain spread to my chest and back. I started hunting around with jerky urgency. The fridge yielded up some milk and a cucumber. An image of Lady Bracknell sprang to mind. I put the cucumber on the pine table. I was getting somewhere. Now, if only I had a knife. A sharp knife and some bread. And butter. Butter, butter, butter – there must be some butter somewhere.

I found the butter. It was rock hard. I put it on the table next to the cucumber. Perhaps it would soften. If I stopped looking so hard for bread I might find it. It was probably somewhere obvious. I put all my nervous energy into the search for a knife. There were plenty of drawers around the kitchen. I pulled them all out. If I could only find a knife I could get on with slicing the cucumber. Paper thin. That would be the hardest part.

I found a bread knife. Still no bread. I applied it cautiously to the cucumber. The serrated edge bit roughly into the green skin, pulping the flesh. Green wetness spread over the scrubbed pine.

The bread was in the pantry, in another fridge. The pantry was the room Fong had gone to for the napkin, and I had gone there looking for a teapot. It was ready-sliced, cold and damp and thick, but it was bread. I left it to thaw out, like the butter. It was now a quarter to five.

In the pantry were many cupboards. I opened them all. All the china a man could wish for was revealed. I chose some with a matching teapot. It was red, white, blue and gold. Served on plates such as these, I felt, my cucumber sandwiches would stand a better chance.

I hacked off the crusts and sliced the butter thick. It was still ice-hard and crumbled rather under the bread knife. I scattered it over the soggy slices, pressing it home with the cucumber. The cucumber was chunkier than I'd hoped, but some judicious squashing thinned things down. I cut the result roughly into quarters and put them on a plate.

I found teabags, but no kettle. In the pantry I noticed a water-fountain similar to one in Henry's kitchen on the beach. It was Arrowhead Spring with an instant-boiling tap. I squirted some over three teabags, nice and strong. I filled the jug with milk and looked for a tray. An old wooden one leaned against the pantry fridge. I liked the look of it.

Somewhere in the distance I heard the doorbell chime. I made a final survey of my handiwork. I was reasonably pleased, all things considedred. I braced my aching shoulders and set off.

Outside the scene of my recent interview I paused before the door, relieved to have found it but foxed by the mechanics of knocking and opening, tray in hand.

I left the tray on a nearby window-seat and returned to the door.

'Come!'

I put my head round, smiling. 'I'll just fetch the – '

'Where's Mother?' She had changed into a dress and sat regally near the window. Her hair, eyes and lips glowed. There was an edge to her voice.

'Er . . .'

'Haven't you let her in?'

Urgent and repeated chiming answered her question.

'I didn't know I – '

'*Get the goddam door!*'

'I, er . . .'

'What's the matter now?'

'I don't know where it is.'

She shot out of her chair and took off through another door. Following anxiously I found we were back in the hall.

She stood fretting by the door. 'Open it, at least.'

I struggled with several catches and latches.

'Please try not to humiliate me any further.'

I gave a last despairing tug. It opened.

A larger, older version of herself stood on the step, wearing a billowing kaftan. The hair was greyish blonde, recently done. The rather reptilian lips, in this case pale-pink pearl, slid back.

'Hi, honey!'

'Hi.' The Beverly Hills ladies embraced.

I kept holding open the door. 'Who's this?'

'This is Paul.'

'How do you do?' I bowed deferentially from the neck.

'Paul is British.'

'Cute.'

They sailed off. 'I coulda died out there.'

'What the hell. You survived.'

I closed the door with difficulty and hurried after them.

'Would you like me to serve tea now, Madam?' I was getting into the part.

'We don't want it next year.'

'Is he the new help?'

Missee eyed me darkly. 'That's a maybe. My mother knows a great deal about etiquette, don't you?'

'I coulda written books.'

'So? What d'you think?'

'I don't like that "Madam"!'

'I hate it!'

'Don't call her Madam, honey. It makes her feel old.'

'Paul's made us a real old-fashioned English tea.'

'Mmmm, I just love those scones.'

'You made scones, did you, honey?'

'I'm afraid not.' I shifted my feet uneasily, more conscious than ever of my clothes.

'Oh, well . . .' The ladies looked at each other and shrugged. 'What the hell.'

Back at the window-seat someone was sitting by my tray – a big muscly teenager with curly black hair and a Grateful Dead T-shirt. In his hand was a sandwich. He spoke with his mouth full. 'Hey, man, these're cool.'

In the event, he was the only one who thought so.

'There's only one left, I'm afraid. Someone ate them.' I stood with bowed head, the tray on a table between mother and daughter.

'My God! who would do that?'

'He said his name was Denver . . .'

'Denver! Get your ass in here!'

'He said he didn't want to come in.' I had tried to persuade him myself, to get me off the hook. He had reluctantly replaced the last sandwich before taking off.

His grandma picked it up by one corner. 'No tea cakes?'

'I'm afraid not.'

She bit it cautiously and handed it to her daughter.

'One of these is enough already!'

The tray was wrong – a horrible old thing. How could you? The Royal Crown Derby China was too formal for two. The tea was tepid and far too strong. There were no napkins, no lemon, no sweet-and-low. There were no teaspoons, no knives or forks.

I passed a defeated hand through my tangled hair, 'Oh, dear. I suppose that's it then.'

'Not a quitter, are you, honey?'

'I think I may just not be cut out for this kind of thing.'

'Mumsy? What do you think?'

'His accent is adorable.'

I got a week's trial and a Mercedes. I was to go get my stuff and return that night.

I drove out to the beach, going all the way along Sunset to Pacific Coast Highway. Henry was out. Jimmy lay on the deck, his baseball cap over his eyes.

'What kind of Mercedes is it?'

'I don't know. Does it matter?'

'Sounds a good gig if you get a Mercedes. You'll probably be able to talk the guy into a movie deal. Captive audience.'

'You don't know what it's like . . .' We stood with my bags by the car.

Jimmy said, 'It's a 350.SE.'

'Oh, well . . .'

'See you on your day off.'

When I reached the outer defences it was dark. I pushed the buttons on my pad as directed. The gate swung open. I hesitated. Was this real? The gate pointed the way. The car slipped forward. I turned down the side drive to the back door. Here there were no castellations, no moat. The door was locked electronically. I had been given the combination. I pushed the buttons. Nothing happened. I pushed them again. Nothing. I stood by the door in the warm night, looking at the bell. Somewhere above me heavy-metal music faintly wailed. Who inside would hear me? I pushed and waited. Five minutes later I pushed again.

'Ayee! Evlybody sleep.' Fong's black hair hung over his angular face. His voice was slurred.

'Sorry, Fong.'

'Vey bad boy.'

'I couldn't make the combination work.'

'You Number Nine!'

'Number nine?'

'Chinese people say, Number Nine. Like a dog!'

'I'm very sorry to wake you.'

'No talkee me. Me talkee you, lookee, lookee.' The back door opened into the kitchen. Fong stood by the pine table, stabbing with a finger. 'Vey bad boy!' The green cucumber stain was plain to see.

Included in the deal was an apartment situated behind the kitchen. Fong grumblingly showed me the way. He left me on the threshold.

'Good night, Fong. Sorry.'

He shook his head as he shuffled away, muttering, 'All butler no good.' I closed the door behind me and switched on the light.

It was black. Black walls, black floor, black sheets on the narrow bed. There was a door through to a tiled bathroom, also black.

I put down my bags and sat on the end of the bed. The heavy-metal noise here was louder. Black curtains framed a full-length window. I looked out.

A castle when it is not a castle is a house in Beverly Hills. Seen from the rear, from the quarters of a servant, the house was large and white and vaguely Spanish.

Here the moat became a palm-fringed pool. At the confluence of these two waterways was a rocky grotto full of turbulent foam. Steam came off it in a multicoloured cloud. Subaquatic disco lights throbbed to the rhythm of the heavy-metal beat. In the midst of it all writhed a human shadow. I watched blankly for a while before drawing the curtains across. They shut out the sight but not the sound.

Turning back into the room I noticed an envelope on my pillow. The envelope was lilac, lined with gold. Inside was a note.

My husband has a breakfast meeting at 6 a.m. Wear a uniform.

It was signed Jayne Belle Graumann.

I tugged listlessly at a cupboard door to see if something suitable might be hanging there. A television set slid out on runners. I lay on the bed, pushing buttons on the box, looking for a movie. Louis Malle's *Black Moon* was just starting on HBO.

I watched for a while, trying to blot out the rest. More and more I felt Malle's obsession with Kathleen Harrison's breasts. I tossed and turned. The music wailed.

I got up, switched off, went to the window. Could I tell a member of the household not to make such an infernal noise? The figure was still writhing. I thought of my six o'clock debut. There was no hope of sleep. I opened the window and stepped out.

Heavily sweating Denver smiled happily when he saw me.

'Hey, dude! What's goin' on?'

'I wondered if you wouldn't mind – '

'Getting settled in?'

'I wouldn't say settled, exactly.'

'You need to relax, bro. Go with the flow.'

'It isn't always easy.'

'It is if you do enough drugs.'

'I think I'm in enough trouble, frankly . . .'

'Here, have a hit.' Denver gestured to a joint and a bottle of Remy Martin.

'Perhaps the brandy . . .'

Denver held out the bottle, 'Come on in, if you like.'

'I've got to get some sleep. I have to be on duty at six.'

'Best way to get to sleep, this.'

'I'd have to find my trunks . . .'

'That's OK. You're not a fag, are you?'

'Certainly not.'

'I didn't think so. Most butlers are fags. The last guy, Jesus! There's no way I would've gotten in here with him.'

'Tracey told me. I feel weird sleeping in his bed.'

'How d'ya like that groovy decor?'

'That's what I mean.'

'My mom's decorator was his boyfriend.'

Day dawned grey, LA smog mixed with mist from the jacuzzi and moat. My final fitful doze lasted too long. Nightmare merged with reality at five-thirty-eight. Neck, shoulder, chest and back pains had spread to my stomach and feet. Five-star cognac glazed my tongue and tonsils. I gagged in the black bathroom, under a cold shower. It was then I remembered the uniform. Muscles tightened my face to a mask of frenzy as I dredged the pine-smelling interiors of the black cupboards. A pair of black nylon trousers reeked of stale perfume. I had no choice. I heaved and hauled them over my thighs, bending double to stretch their waist around mine. Stuffing my shorts to one side, closing my mind to disease, I tugged the thin nylon zip almost to the top.

Breathing with difficulty I encased my torso in a white

mess-jacket. It had brass buttons. I had to do them all up to prevent my shirt from bulging above the trousers.

Looking in the mirror, making final adjustments to my black, elasticated bow-tie, I remembered my shoes. I watched my face go from red to white to red. Not only did I not think I could bend down to put them on, I only had my sneakers. They too were red and white, and very worn. But as Kenny Graumann would say, or 'Sir' as I had to call him now, what the hell. I pulled them on somehow and headed stiffly for the kitchen.

'Ayee! Vey bad boy. Vey late!' Fong sat at the pine table, serrating the rim of a grapefruit.

'Sorry, Fong.'

'Number nine.'

'What can I do to help?'

'Evlybody butler lay table. I no can do it.'

'Lay the table?'

'Hully up. People coming.'

'But where is the table?'

'Ayee! Talkee talkee talkee, no good.'

'Yes, but I don't know where it is!'

'*Dining loom*!' Fong's yellow face shifted down several shades.

'But *where is* the dining room? I don't know *where it is*!'

'I think I made a pretty good job of decorating this room, Kenny. Would you deny that?' Boothby Cunningham described an extravagant arc with one long pale hand, passing it through his long pale hair on the way. His clothes hung loose on his long, languid frame, linens and silks of the most natural hues. A yellow silk handkerchief protruded from one cuff.

Until two minutes to six I'd never seen the place. I hadn't had time to take it in. We all looked around. My own view was partially obstructed by the rood-screen behind which I stood, coffee-pot in hand. It was Tudor Baronial, judging by the low, blackened beams and a dominant painting of Henry

VIII. Kenny Graumann sat at one end of a long refectory table. Boothby Cunningham was at the other. I hadn't known how else to set them.

'This room I like,' Kenny conceded. 'This is my kinda room.' He was wearing the same jacket he'd worn at the beach. His cigar-case rested by his plate.

'It's a masculine room, Kenny.' Boothby gestured dramatically with his hand on the word 'masculine'.

Kenny bared his teeth. 'Jayne Belle hates this room.'

Boothby smiled conspiratorially, 'We can't let Jayne Belle have her way all the time.'

Kenny looked belligerent. 'Can't we?'

'Kenny, listen to me. This new project is not in the strict sense of the word mere decoration.'

'It's not?' For a moment Kenny looked hopeful.

'We are going far beyond that, far, far beyond.'

'Wherever it is, I hope there's money there.'

'We are talking art here, Kenny. Art.'

'I am *not* building the Sistine Chapel in my house. More coffee over here.'

I hurried across with the burning pot, trying to think of Jeeves. Kenny glanced up, I thought curiously, as I poured. Boothby was saying, 'Listen to me, in this very town . . . Are you listening?' Kenny shook his head. 'Right here in the City of the Angels, an artist who is literally the reincarnation of Michelangelo!'

Kenny stopped shaking his head. He leaned forward tensely. I noticed the pigskin briefcase next to his chair. 'You listen to me, Boothby. I have to take crap all day long at the studio. Gimme a break at breakfast.'

A door opened at the far end of the room. Framed in it, Jayne Belle Graumann in a grey sweatsuit and red headband. Behind her a musclebound giant in blue.

'We're on our way down to the gym.' She snaked across to Kenny and perched on his knee. 'Hi, how're you guys gettin' . . . *My God!*' she screeched, '*Paul!!*'

I crept out from behind my screen, 'Yes, Madam?'

'What is this? What in hell is this!?'

'I'm sorry, I don't – '

'The Spode, goddammit, the Spode!'

Boothby Cunningham glanced around and looked me up and down. 'I thought it was a little strange.'

'Spode at breakfast. My God!'

'I'm sorry.' I gritted my teeth. 'I didn't know.'

Boothby trailed his fingers across his brow. 'Poor David, he'd just die if he could . . .'

'What was wrong with the Royal Crown Derby?'

'Yesterday – '

'And there's no ice-water, no salt, no ashtrays, no flowers . . .'

At last Jayne Belle took her hot eyes off me. 'How've you two boys been getting along?' Her voice was saccharin sweet.

'Kenny can't see it.'

She turned her husband's face around. 'What can't you see, sweetie-pie?'

Kenny said, 'I gotta go.'

'I told him about Massimo.' Boothby had his elbows on his end of the table.

'And?'

'Nothing.'

'What's the matter with you?' Jayne Belle rose from her husband's knee as if from a plague-spot. 'Have you no imagination? No taste?'

'I guess not.'

'You never made one movie that wasn't shit. Now you got the chance to make the greatest movie of all time and you can't see it.'

'No one said anything to me about any movie.'

'Boothby?'

'He didn't give me a chance.'

She sat back on his lap, one arm around his neck. 'Kenny, honey, listen to me. Recreating the Sistine Chapel here in this house will be the greatest celluloid experience in the history of Hollywood.'

'They already made a Michelangelo picture. With Chuck Heston. It was lousy.'

'D'you have to spend your whole life trying to mortify me? Have you any idea how much *work* Booboo here has put in on this project?'

Kenny shook his head. 'Honey, I gotta go. I'll be late. Can I borrow your car? Mine's in the shop.'

'Absolutely not. I got things to do.'

He looked at me. 'Then this guy here'll have to take me. Can you drive?'

'I need him here, dammit. He's got *work* to do.'

'He can do it when he gets back.'

In the Mercedes I caught Kenny's eye in the mirror.

'Have you thought at all about my movie?'

'Huh?'

'The skating picture. Remember?'

'My God! Is there anyone in this town doesn't want something from me?'

'I was hoping perhaps . . .'

'Last night it was Tracey, draying me to get a limousine. Here. Stop here.' We were still in Beverly Hills, heading south on Palm.

'Not going to the studio, Sir?'

'I have to see somebody.'

Shaking his head, muttering, 'Limousines, Michelangelo, God help me . . .' gripping the pigskin case, he jumped out and disappeared into a maze of manicured lawns.

I loaded a silver tray with iced tea and found my way down to the basement. The olympic-size gym shimmered with equipment. As I descended I could hear Tracey's voice. 'Mom, don't you think we need a limo? Nearly all my friends got limos.'

'Whatever.'

Tracey in spandex hung from a crossbeam in metal boots. I caught her upside-down eye. 'Don't you think we need a limo, Paul?

'Paul! Where the hell've you been!?' Her mother lay face-down on a mat. Above her the muscle-man was busy twisting one leg up her back.

'I had to drive your husband. I'm sorry.'

'You didn't have to take all day.'

Tracey said, 'If we had a limo Paul would never need to leave the house.'

I considered this. 'I don't think Mister Graumann would like it.'

Jayne Belle's twisted sideways face looked interested. 'Oh, no? What makes you say that?'

'He said so just now.'

'Is that a fact?'

The doorbell chimed and I hurried to answer it. It was Jayne Belle's mother. She had brought me the complete set of *Upstairs, Downstairs* videos. 'Take a look at these, honey. They'll help.'

A few days later a brand-new Cadillac limousine arrived. It was stretched to fully sixty feet. At the wheel, clad in a uniform infinitely more form-fitting than my own, was Doctor Love.

— 3 —

The weeks passed. Days and nights merged in a blur of meals and duties. The days off spoken of by Jimmy never seemed to materialise. Something in my performance made it indispensable round the clock. My position was confirmed as 'permanent'. Something in the word chilled my blood.

I thought the incredible salary might cheer Natasha up, so I called her. The big hollow Hall had one telephone only. I let it ring and ring until a voice said, 'Hallo?'

I said, 'Hallo,' as well, guardedly, knowing who it was but hoping to be mistaken.

'Hallo. This is Lady Roxbury.'

'Can I speak to Natasha, please?'

'Is that Nigel?' The line was remarkably clear.

'This is Paul.'

'Oh. I thought you were in America.'

'I am in America.'

'Isn't ringing up from there terribly expensive?'

'I've got some rather good news actually.'

'Hold on. I'll see if I can find her. She's been out a lot recently.'

The line went hollow for an age while the dollars racked up. I might at any moment be summoned to duty, and my agitation had taken me almost to breaking point when my wife's voice piped up. 'Hallo?'

'Natasha?'

'Hi.'

'Good news.'

'Oh, good.'

'I've landed this amazing job.'

'Great. What about our ten thousand?'

'You won't *believe* the salary.'

'Is the ten thousand OK?'

'It's almost a *thousand* dollars a week!'

'Fantastic. What about . . .'

'I'll be wiring it over to you through the bank.'

'What? The ten thousand!'

'No. The salary. Every two weeks or so. You'll be rich! The difference between . . .'

'You still haven't said about the ten thousand.'

'The ten thousand's tied up at the moment.'

'Tied up? How do you mean? Not in one of your deals?'

'I can't explain the details now. It's a movie deal. They take a while to – '

'Oh, *God*, Paul, how *could* you? That's *everything* we had in the world. We've got *nothing* now.' The word 'nothing' was a sob.

'Don't be silly, Natasha. My salary . . .'

'Shut up about your stupid salary. You'll probably get fired tomorrow.'

'God, Natasha . . .'

'You won't last a month and you'll owe it all in phone bills. I've got to go.'

'But the chap I'm working for is the movie chap who . . . Natasha?'

But she had hung up. The empty transatlantic hum mocked my brave spiel.

As I replaced the receiver the intercom squawked: 'Paul! Where the hell areya?'

'Coming, Sir.'

*

Doctor Love introduced me to his tailor. We drove there together in the limo. 'A bit different to the last time you drove me, eh, Love?'

'Thass right, British. You life got direction now.'

We had decided to model my new uniform on Ralph Richardson's in *Fallen Idol*. It seemed appropriate. It needed to be ready in time for the party. The Sistine Chapel project was to be launched in style, with no expense spared. The theme was fifteenth-century Italian. Uncompromising authenticity was the keynote of our preparations. Exhaustive consultations were convened in the kitchen between Fong, myself and Boothby Cunningham.

'You must know all about the Renaissance, Paul?' The word 'renaissance' provoked one of Boothby's most extravagant gestures.

'Not really, no.'

'Being European, surely . . .'

'I am not European. I'm British. English, in fact.'

'At least I thought you'd know if it happened in the fifteenth century.'

Fifteenth-century flowers were almost as much of a mystery as fifteenth-century food. On the Wednesday before the Saturday of the party Doctor Love and I drove to the flower market in downtown LA. We left at 5 a.m. Somewhere over the desert the sun was rising, striking the downtown buildings as we hit the Harbor Freeway, making them look like Manhattan. Downtown had a nuked, empty look. Bums lay in doorways. The one-way system and the early hour foxed Love for a while, but when we reached Seventh and Grand it was still only five-thirty. We parked the limo and entered the huge wholesale flower warehouse.

'I suppose the flowers in the fifteenth century were pretty well the same as they are today?' I looked hopefully at Doctor Love, who was examining a cluster of red-hot pokers.

'Man, these look good.'

'But would you say reminiscent of fifteenth-century Rome?'

'Them ancient Roman cats, man, they was mean.' He took a poker plant and waggled it. 'Right up you honky ass.'

'That's how they killed Edward the second. Wait a minute!' something Royal stirred my mind. I headed for a salesperson. She was a bubble-haired heavyweight with glasses, busy making a fantastically complex bow out of red ribbon.

Her smile snapped on, 'How can I help you this morning?' Her voice was small and sharp, pitched high and sugary.

'Can you tell me . . .' I smiled with similar insincerity, '. . . is the lily of the valley the same as the fleur-de-lys?'

We loaded the lilies of the valley into a box, charged them to Kenny's account, carried them out between us to the car. A thousand stems at a dollar a stem. Doctor Love agreed it was a bold plan.

'You better be right though. This shit's *expensive*.'

They were small, too. I spent most of the morning finding things small enough to put them in, the afternoon arranging them tastefully about the place. They didn't make much of a splash, their subtle message lost in the cubic vastness. I felt the now familiar panic rising. Worst of all, their cute little bells were becoming noticeably droopy. Like me, they seemed depressed by their surroundings.

Around five the doorbell chimed alarmingly. I raced for the hall. I had been on duty twelve hours. Six to go if I was lucky. I hauled the thing open with my customary half-bow. It was Jayne Belle.

'Hi, honey!' She seemed in a good mood. I tingled with relief. If I could only keep her that way.

'Hallo,' I oozed, bowing lower, raised face wreathed in a smarmy smile.

'Well?' She posed before me with Al Jolson hands. My chest pains locked in as my eyes flickered warily from coif to thousand-dollar toe. It might be anything.

'Very nice.' The smarmy smile melded into a gallant leer.

'You like it?'

'Love it!'

— 53 —

'What, exactly?'

'Everything about you.' I didn't have to think. There was never time.

'You couldn't make it to the flower market?' Her smile froze as she looked around.

'Absolutely!'

'You coulda fooled me.'

'Ah, well. Step this way and I'll escort you into the fifteenth century.' But it was no use. My heart wasn't in it. My showmanship had the hollow ring of doom. We peered together into alcoves at the diminutive display. The Dauphin's famous fleurs, if such they really were, seemed only to wilt further before Jayne Belle's dreadful scrutiny.

I wilted in my turn when at last she rounded on me. 'Let's get this straight. You bought *all* lily of the valley?'

'Yes.'

'Nothing else?'

'Nothing.'

'How many stems?'

'Er . . .'

'How MANY!?'

'A thousand.'

'My *God*! You know what they cost?'

'I'm afraid I do, yes.'

'You know how long they last?'

'Er . . .'

'Twenty-four hours, goddammit! Most of these are dead already. You will be too when my husband finds out.'

Kenny had designed his office to intimidate movie stars and directors. It did a pretty good job on me. The scale and general theme was 'Roman Collosal'. I knocked and entered. Great Men of History, admired by Kenny for their iron will, stood around with cold marble sneers as I crossed to his desk. I caught Napoleon's eye and found myself humming a brave hymn: 'Onward Christian soldiers . . .' Kenny sat impassively behind his huge marble desk, watching me through his glittering glasses.

'What is it, Paul?' Only a gold clock with an Imperial eagle separated us. I proffered my copy of that morning's flower bill.

'Your wife asked me to show you this, Sir.'

He looked down at it and up at me. 'I don't understand.'

'Flowers for the party. You know, this weekend.'

He studied it for some moments, shaking his head.

'I was thinking of the fifteenth century, you see . . .'

Kenny's fist came down. The Imperial clock jumped perceptibly on its gilded claws. He lowered his head to the marble, then raised it again and gazed at me fixedly. As his mouth opened my eyes closed.

'Goddam Sistine Chapel. I'm a Zionist for Chrissakes!'

I opened my eyes with what I hoped was a deeply sympathetic look.

'You a Catholic?' Kenny asked dangerously.

'No, Sir.'

'No?'

'Church of England.'

'OK. Church of England. You wouldn't like it if I asked you to build a goddam synagogue in the middle of *your* house, would you?'

'I haven't got a house.'

'Imagine if you did.'

I could. 'I suppose not.'

Kenny shook his head and his glasses glinted balefully. 'Art.'

'Sir?'

'Art's my problem. Always has been. Every time you make a buck some smartass starts draying you about art.'

Certainly art was central to the party. On Friday Jayne Belle's mother, Iris, made a return trip to the flower market. Dr Love drove in a strictly non-executive role. I took the blame squarely for the lilies (they were all dead by now) but Jayne Belle saw no reason not to lay some on Love. Blame, a near relative of Guilt, should be doled out as evenly as possible, she felt. Being black did not excuse Love from human failings in her eyes. He marched into the pantry as jauntily as he could under the burden of her mother's selections. He managed a wink at me. With a hoarse cry Fong leapt into urgent production of iced tea as Iris collapsed onto a kitchen chair. She was steaming like a kettle. She touched her fingertips to her damp brow, patted around her hairdo. She fixed me with a childlike look.

'Do I look like the wreck of the *Hesperus*?'

'You look fabulous. Honestly. Fresh as a daisy.'

Fong dumped down her glass of iced tea. 'Look vey *hot*.'

'Isn't he just adorable?' She looked up at me, then him. 'Fong, has this got sweet'n'low?'

'Ayeee!' He snatched it back.

Iris waited until he was back in the kitchen before saying, 'Asshole!'

We spent the afternoon together arranging the flowers. A skill all good domestics must master, she confided.

My fingers crumbling oasis, I said, 'You should start a training school.'

'Don't get cute, honey.'

'No, honestly . . .'

'You really think so? I could sure use some extra cash.'

'Really? I thought, I mean . . .'

'Don't be fooled.' Iris shook her head over a cluster of orchids. 'That dirty ratfink, my ex. Thirty-six years of marriage.'

'Good Lord. I wouldn't've thought – '

'Look. Forget the crap. He dumped me for a bimbo of seventeen, OK?'

'Golly. I am sorry.'

'Not half as sorry as me. When I divorced him he disguised his assets.'

'Unlike her, eh?'

'It isn't funny, Paul.'

'No. Absolutely not.'

'My daughter still speaks to him. Kenny does deals with him, when it suits him. There's no loyalty.'

'What does he do?'

'He's in pictures. You'll see him soon enough. He's coming to the party.'

'How awful for you. Will he bring the bimbo?'

Iris's jewelled hands throttled a chrysanthemum with a piece of green ribbon. 'That little harlot. She's long gone. But there's always another. Let's not discuss it, honey. It's too painful.'

'Absolutely.'

'The dirty rat. I'll get him one day.'

Napkin folding is another artistic thing. Jayne Belle herself took charge of me in this. She showed me a book with diagrams.

'I think we should do fans. Do you think we should do fans?' She looked at me intently.

'Absolutely.'

'You don't care, do you?'

'Of course I care.'

'Don't they have fabulous parties in England?'

'Certainly.'

'With gorgeous place settings?'

'I suppose I never paid too much attention . . .'

'Well now's the time to start, honey.'

She left me in the entry hall, alone with the manual and ten circular tables, each set for ten. Each setting required a fan. There was mockery in those naked tablecloths, each one bare but for its artistic quota of flowers. Twenty minutes in found me wanting, wilting at the spine much as my few "fans" wilted lopsidely at their places. I heard footsteps approaching from the kitchen. My nervous neck and butler's back locked into familiar spasm. Even as I held my breath one of my fans subsided onto its back, utterly undone.

It was Rojay. It was the first time I'd ever been glad to see him.

'Hi Rojay.'

Rojay strolled over, hands thrust deep in the pockets of his pleated pants. He stood beside me contemplatively for a moment, looking down at the table. He removed one hand from his pants, crooked a perfumed arm around my aching neck. 'Hi, sweetypie.'

'What d'you think?'

'What I think about what, babydoll?'

'About my fans.'

'I think . . .' Languidly he backflipped a couple of them over. They offered no resistance. 'What's this?' He held up Jayne Belle's book of *Total Table Etiquette* by one corner. 'What's this garbage?'

'For fuck sake, Rojay . . .'

'What are you afraid of? That bitch?'

Really, this was too much. 'She's *not* a bitch. You mustn't speak like that Rojay, honestly.' My ears flapped desperately.

Rojay smiled with lazy contempt. 'She's not?'

Familiar heels clicked in the passage. The proof, as the Americans say, is in the pudding.

'What's goin' on?' Jayne Belle held an iced tea in one hand and a chicken wing in the other, '*Rojay*, honey. Nobody told me you were here . . .' She looked at me accusingly.

Rojay squeaked across the parquet to her in a series of wiggling disco gyrations. He encircled her in his chubby arms and waggled her to and fro.

'Jayne Belle. You *gorgeous* bitch . . .' His black eyes locked into my startled ones. He poked out his tongue. 'I've just been telling Paul here what shit that silly old book of yours is.'

'Not my fabulous placement book!'

'Total shit.'

'Oh, honey, c'mon.'

'Forget it, babe. It's yesterday's news, swear to God.'

'Oh, well, what the hell. It's just some old book Mumsy gave me. Paul, honey,' her voice was sweet as molasses, 'how're those fans comin' along?'

'Er . . .'

'I told Paul to forget about the fans.' Rojay blew me a kiss. I almost felt like blowing one back. I grinned weakly. 'Yes, I . . .' I looked down at the tumbled linen on the table next to me.

'Goddammit, Rojay! Paul is *my* butler. He gets his orders from *me*.'

'OK, fine. Have it your own way.' Rojay raised his hands and rolled his eyes to heaven. 'You want fans at your party, fine. Something artistic, you tell me. Lots of artsy fartsy people comin' from the museum an' what not. Boothby say he want fifteenth-century food, fine. I am *sure* they folded their napkins like fans in the fifteenth century. Oh, *sure*.'

'Paul, honey, why don't you go and see how Hoobey and Werner are getting along in the marquee? Rojay and I need to talk.'

A marquee was being erected behind the house, approximating to the site where the Sistine Chapel would eventually be reproduced. It took up most of the garden, apart from the pool. Beyond the pool, from the marquee, immediately outside my bedroom window, a wooden stage was taking shape. I strolled through the debris of wood-shavings and ladders. Late California sun baked through the striped canvas. Another day in paradise was drawing to a close. I was relieved to have escaped from Jayne Belle and her fans. A butler lives his life from minute to minute, on his toes, on his nerves, on his wits, alert as a gazelle. At the end of the day, if it ever does end, he is happy to have just survived. Even then the crises, never far away, tend to inhabit his dreams. I could see at a glance, the next crisis would be the marquee. It was impossible to believe it would be ready by tomorrow. If it wasn't it would be my fault.

There was an edge to my voice as I called out, 'Hoobey!'

'Yes sir, boss!'

I looked up, massaging my neck and flexing my back. Hoobey

was balanced high above on a plank propped between two tall stepladders. He wore a faded, lumberjack workshirt and grey, workhorse jeans. Round his waist was his battered leather toolbelt. A patina of dust clung as usual to everything from his grizzly grey hair to his stout workboots. Hoobey's task in life was to redeem sinners by employing them on his workforce, to work tirelessly towards goals of self-improvement, but above all to make and keep Jayne Belle and Kenny Graumann happy. In this he and I were as one. His great pleasure in life was to leap to obey my slightest command, seeing in me and my uniform the executive arm of absolute power. We were both happy with the ironies and enjoyed our roles. After all, although technically beneath me, he was freer. He could go home nights.

'I find it hard to believe that this could possibly be ready for tomorrow.'

Hoobey chuckered his head to one side, smiling a tight, lopsided American smile, indicating true grit. 'Donchoo go frettin', now, y'hear.'

The guttural voice of Werner came from down in one corner, where he was crouched over a grey metal box full of wires. 'Paul's right. How can I work with all this shit? All this American electrical stuff is junk.'

I clutched my back at the waistline of my black, butler's jacket, and flexed my tired, pinstriped knees.

'Somethin' botherin' you there, Paul?' Hoobey was at my side in seconds. He got my head between his hands and looked into my eyes in the full healing posture.

'Not lettin' it get to you now, boss?'

'No, no. It's OK.'

'Have you been listening to the tape?' Hoobey had lent me one of his life-enhancement tapes: one listen to be well on the road to a fulfilled life.

'Er . . . I've been rather busy. You know how it is.'

'Remember what we said about *making* time, about getting in *control* of your own life?'

'Those tapes are shit. You may as well sit in the bathroom and masturbate.' Werner had risen from his corner, an easy smile on his face. He looked fulfilled enough considering how far he was from the Fatherland. He was a stocky fellow with a healthy, glowing face, chubby, ruddy cheeks, curly blond hair.

'Now lookee here, Werner.' Hoobey gave him his most down-home grin. 'Everyone's entitled to their own opinion. You know I'm the first to admit to that . . .'

'Shit. Just like everything else in America. Look at this junk I'm supposed to work with.' He held up a tiny fuse. 'The only reason that cheap bastard buys this junk is because it's cheap. Then he expects me to work miracles with it. Everyone knows the only decent electrical equipment comes from Germany, but no. Graumann has to buy this junk. Cheap bastard.'

'Who's calling me a cheap bastard?'

My shoulders went into spasm but it was only Boothby Cunningham. He wore a long woollen scarf of many bright colours. He gaped around the tent for a long silent moment, mouth open wide with affected languorous dismay. He tossed the scarf over one shoulder, finally clutched his brow. 'My God!'

Werner growled, 'This is all we need.'

Hoobey said, 'Howdee there, Boothby. How are you today?'

'You do realise the unveiling is tomorrow?' Boothby ignored the question, but there was a wild surmise in his eyes and hair.

'Sho'nuff, boss.'

'And that Massimo di Los Angeles will be here in the morning to set up his *fabulous* artwork?'

'No sweat.'

'Possibly the world's Greatest Living Artist?'

'Absolutely!'

'And that *my entire* reputation is riding on this affair?'

'We wouldn't want anything untoward happening to *that*, Boothby. No siree.'

'You're damn right you don't, you moron.'

'Steady on now, Boothby.' Hoobey tilted his head back, his

jaw forward, still smiling. Over in the corner I heard Werner mutter something guttural.

'You'll never work in this town again!' Boothby was getting white around the mouth. I felt it was time to step in. Peacekeeping is a time-honoured tradition among butlers.

'It's all right, Boothby.'

'What!' He swung violently to face me.

'It'll be ready on time. Don't worry. Leave it to me.' I spoke with a confidence I was far from feeling, trying hard to infuse my voice with as much of the Admirable Crighton spirit as I could muster.

At this moment we were interrupted by a deceptively effusive 'Hi!' from the tent entrance. It started high on the high note, then sank to a low note that was close to a threat. We had been successfully sneaked up on by Kenny.

'Hi, Kenny!' Boothby's hi was more effusive still, without the low note. He held out his arms, like a girl who wants to hug her long-lost sheepdog.

'How's it going?' Kenny beamed around the devastation, inscrutable behind his twinkling glasses.

'Oh, pretty good, Kenny. It's goin' good.' Hoobey chucked his jaw grittily. In the corner Werner grunted.

'Kenny, it's going *beautifully* . . .' Boothby flung his scarf round his throat for sheer unfettered joy. 'Everything is just *divine* and *fabulous*!'

'Good evening, Sir.' I bowed slightly from the aching waist.

Kenny was smiling a non-smile and nodding up and down. Something in his air of satisfaction told me we were for it. 'What this place needs is statues.'

Some of the effusiveness faded from Boothby's face. 'Huh?' His mouth remained open.

'This guy's a sculptor, isn't he?'

'No, Kenny,' Boothby marshalled his facial forces, ready for the fray. 'He's not.'

'Michelangelo was a sculptor, right?'

'Michelangelo Vespucci,' Boothby Cunningham's pale hands

cut exquisite figures in the air, 'was a many-faceted artist, the *ultimate* Renaissance man. His vision of the Male Form . . .' Boothby laid one hand across his brow and closed his eyes . . .

'Arright arready. He made statues, right?'

Boothby shook his head in slow despair. 'Right, Kenny. He made statues.'

'Ya gotta dress the set, believe me. What this joint needs is statues.'

'But, Kenny . . .' Boothby's hands wrung his scarf.

'What I see right here in the middle is "Victor of Lodi".'

'Victor of Lodi' is Napoleon in bronze on a horse. It weighed seven tons. I looked at Hoobey. His jaw was setting grimly. Our objections, not that we were in a position to have any, were different to Boothby's. Both hands dropped his scarf and clutched his hair.

'Not Napoleon! Kenny, I implore you . . .'

'And what is wrong with Napoleon?' Kenny was looking dangerous.

'Kenny. Kenny, sweetheart,' Boothby smoothed his hair over his ears. He spoke patiently. 'Napoleon Bonaparte did not *live* in the fifteenth century.'

'Paul here can do some of his stuff.'

I shuffled my feet modestly. It was a favourite ritual of ours when there was 'company'.

'How does that one go, Paul?' Kenny looked at me keenly.

'Which one, Sir?' I oozed.

'You know. The impossible one.'

' "Impossible is only a word", Sir, "to the coward a refuge, to the timid a ghost, but, believe me, in the mouth of power . . ." '

'No! No! No!' Boothby collapsed onto the bottom step of one of Hoobey's ladders.

'A Declaration of Impotence!' crowed Kenny. Boothby burst into tears.

In the end we settled for Julius Caesar. At least he was Italian. Also horseless, weighing in at a mere ton and a half.

All through the night the work buzzed and banged on,

the marquee arclights reflected hellishly from the pool onto my black bedroom walls. After serving dinner and waiting patiently at my post till after midnight for the last guests to leave. I had cleared the debris, snuffed dozens of candles in their high wall-brackets with my long (fabulous antique) snuffing rod, and fallen face downward on my bed. I had been tippling Poire Williams in my pantry during the latter stages to keep me going. Once horizontal the stuff wouldn't quit. The dark, flickering room heaved queasily, like an old tub rocking on an oily sea.

Some time later my nightmares were interrupted. I came from half- to three-quarters conscious with a start. Someone's head was whispering, just inside my door.

'Hey dude, whas goin' on?'

'Go away, Denver.'

'Not flaking, Red?' Denver called me Red Butler. Something to do with my complexion under pressure.

'Sleeping.'

'In your clothes?' Denver had turned on the light. 'Hey, guys, come'n say hi to the Red Butler.' I pulled a black pillow over my head and groaned. Denver sat down heavily beside me, pushed something cold into my neck. 'What you need is a little wakener.'

Denver and the Hot Hebrews, his band, had returned after chucking-out time at the Central on Sunset, a club where rotten bands like them can play for nothing on Friday nights. They had discovered bottles of champagne in the pantry fridge, Taittinger 'Compte de Champagne', Kenny's favourite, which could easily be missed. As well as this the guys were in possession of two chicks – the sort who hang out at the Central on Friday nights. Their names were Michelle and Lulu. They could really appreciate a fine mansion, but they had never met a real butler, not a British one, anyway. I struggled onto one elbow, not wishing to let the side down. The presence of chicks gave an edge to everyone's performance. There was angst in the air of my room.

In designing the apartment for my predecessor, Boothby had thoughtfully installed a top-of-the-line sound system. Into the works of this, one of the guys inserted a Grateful Dead tape.

'Let's jam!'

'Right on, let's party!' One of the guys lit a joint and passed it to Michelle and Lulu.

'Denver, honestly . . .' Feebly I went through the motions of protest.

'Take it easy, dude. We have to rehearse.'

'Can't you do it somewhere else?' Michelle and Lulu were inspecting my black marble bathroom, finding it awesome.

'But this is like the green room for tomorrow, man,' pointing to the window, 'there's the stage. Right there.'

'I still don't see . . .'

'Hey, Red, you gotta mirror somewhere around here?' Marvin, smallest of the guys, with tight blond curls and the face of a cherub, held up a small envelope made from a page of a glossy magazine.

'Here's one!' Lulu, in the bathroom was quick to respond. She appeared holding my shaving mirror, smiling. She had red nails, red hair and a Southern whine. She was from somewhere in North Carolina, a small town. She worked as a secretary in an office in Beverly Hills. Her boss was young guy, but *really* nice, ya know? She wore hotpants. Her legs weren't great.

'Hey, mister butler man, I could just die in your tub. Die 'n go to heaven.' Her voice was gravelly, sexy. She brushed by me on cowboy boots and delivered the mirror to Marvin. She watched him hungrily as he dumped the contents of the envelope on to the glass and got to work on it with his credit card.

After I had fetched glasses and made sure my guests lacked for nothing I lay down on the sofa in my sitting-room – a wall away from the Gerry Garcia licks. Exhaustion and anxiety fought for a while over my carcase. Finally exhaustion won.

I came to with a start, crumpled and smelly, deeply disturbed. Smoggy morning light gleamed balefully on the cheap luxury of the room. I could hear distant kitchen noises. I didn't need to look at my watch to know I was in trouble. At least I was dressed. I headed for the bathroom for a head soak and a twenty-second scrape. I was late. To appear unshaven to boot would be to stand guilty as charged. It would be written all over my face. The successful butler must never appear at a disadvantage. To serve well one must always seem in command. What he does and when he does it, is not the important point, but *how* he does it. Or how he appears to do it. Appearances, particularly in Beverly Hills, are all that really count. My mind raced. My bedroom was wrecked but deserted. I picked up my shaving mirror, smudgy but scraped clean. Through the window the marquee operations were in full swing. That was something, at least. I hurried to the bathroom.

'Hi, hun!' Lulu lay in the tub, her red hair tied up, still smiling.

'Good God!'

'Denver said y'all wouldn't mind,' she crooned coyly. There were bubbles in the water, but not many.

'But . . .'

'Wah's matter, darlin',' Lulu sat up, cupping her breasts demurely in her hands. 'I don't embarrass you, do I?'

'It's not that,' I was too freaked out to be embarrassed, or even aroused, 'it's just they mustn't find you here, that's all.'

'Who d'you mean? This is your apartment, isn't it?'

'It's in *their* house.'

'You mean Denver's folks? That's all cool. Denver invited me to stay for the party.'

'*What!*' I glanced at the hotpants in the corner. If Jayne Belle and her mother had a worst fear it was this.

'Whassa matter, butler man,' Lulu stretched one leg out of the water and arched her foot, 'not good enough for these fine folks?' It wasn't the greatest leg in the world, but pink and steamy in the black faux marble atmosphere it got my gallantry up. Butlers are human, after all.

'I'm sure you're very good, Lulu. It's just that here you are, a young girl, stark naked, in my room. I'm sure it will come to me, but right now I wouldn't know how to explain you.'

I chewed my knuckle, looking thoughtfully back at the hotpants, wondering how I could smuggle her out. Aloud, I said, 'What would you wear?'

'That's all fixed. Denver said you could get me in as a waitress.'

'He's coming on his own, Mumsy, sweartagod. I spoke seriously to him this morning.'

'That rat. You can't believe a word he says.'

'If he arrives with one of his harlots, he'll be thrown out.'

'I don't want to be humiliated.'

'You won't be, Mumsy. Would I allow that? Paul, where the *hell* are you going?'

'To the beauty shop.' Jayne Belle and her mother intended spending most of the day before the party at the Yves Santa Barbara Salon of Beauty on South Beverly Drive. I was driving them in my Mercedes since, after a fight, it was decided that Kenny would take Doctor Love and the limo to the studio. Kenny had won the fight by saying, 'What's Paul doing? He's so busy he can't spare the time to drive you?'

I had spent a taxing five minutes rendering my car immaculate and dust free. I had at last found Hoobey and got him to move his truck which was blocking me in. I had put him officially in charge until my return – 'Yes, sir, boss!' I had rushed into the kitchen, where a pitched battle was in progress between Rojay, three of his cherubs, and Fong, who was backed up by a group of his relatives from Chinatown. Although Rojay was officially 'catering' the party, certain dishes had been delegated to Fong. This precarious compromise had been concocted by Jayne Belle, to spare Fong's feelings, feelings which, it seemed to me, though expressed in Chinese, were running high. His yellow complexion had turned a dangerous ochre, his facial angles alarmingly acute. He stood before the oven, flanked by the relatives, all ready for death before the dishonour of allowing Rojay access to it. My arrival created a diversion. Both turned on me and gibbered until I said, 'Look, I have to go into town *now*.'

Even as I spoke Jayne Belle's voice floated through the halls: 'For Chrissakes where *are* you . . .'

At this stage Fong and Rojay buried the hatchet long enough to give me their shopping lists. Both had forgotten vital ingredients. Neither had a pen. I rushed to my room to find one. Lulu lay peacefully in my bed, red hair on the black pillow, her smile childlike in sleep. I had changed from my apron into my jacket. I found pen and paper. I scribbled in a fever while Fong and Rojay continued to recall things. I started the car, pulled round to the front, held open the door, mustered an unctuous smile . . .

'Why are we on Rodeo?'

'I was just going to make a left on Santa Monica, then – '

'Why not just go down Beverly in the first place?'

'I thought this would be quicker.' I tried to minimise the sullenness in my voice.

'Whatever.' Jayne Belle was resigned to suffering. 'It's too late now, anyways.'

I dropped my charges and helped them into the effusive arms of the beauticians. They were both looking *fabulous* already, was it fair to be asked to improve on perfection? Oh, my God, etc., etc . . .

I would pick them up in five hours unless they called. 'Mind you don't forget about us, honey!' Jayne Belle wanted us to part on a cooing note. I guffawed with the best of them at the unlikeliness of this eventuality and drove back across Wilshire to park free in the city parking lot on Beverly. I hoofed the extra mile to Phil's where I stood in line for some time trying to decipher what I had written on my little bit of paper. It was too small for everything Fong and Rojay had wanted. And the writing got smaller and smaller in the corners. Phil's sold chicken and fish at fancy prices, but they were fresh out of wings. They were out of crawfish too. I crossed these off Fong's and Rojay's lists respectively, and pushed on to Gelsons. I couldn't find a parking space at Gelson's so I drove around and around the parking lot, listening to KMET and KROQ. It felt good. When I finally did find a space I stayed on in the car, running the air-conditioning, listening to KMET and KROQ and KLOS, eating a bag of crabmeat I'd bought at Phil's. That was about as good as it got, being a butler.

It was a dreamy blue southern Californian afternoon. I pushed my cart around Gelson's. Everything looked rich and overpriced, the people and the goods. It was very relaxing. People are nice in Gelson's, helping each other out, standing aside in the lanes, talking about pasta, and Granny Smiths, and strawberry shortcake. There is no meanness. Nobody cares too much about the cost of anything. It's soothing, unreal, cut off from squalor. Feeling generous, I got Denver a stack of cans of his favourite Sam Smith's Special Peculiar, and a bottle of Stoly.

I unloaded my cart into the trunk of my car then strolled through the shopping mall to See's Candy. Everyone seemed carefree, on a roll, wearing shorts, spending. I felt stuffy in striped trousers, loosened my pepper-and-salt tie, thought about freedom. Would I ever get out of this? I sent most of my cheque home every month. Natasha and her mother were happy about that. Jayne Belle and her mother were happy. Looking around, most people I could see looked happy. In Beverly Hills time never seems to move forward. The weather never changes. The seasons never change. The fashionable restaurants never change. If you came back in ten years time now would be like yesterday: the same movie. You can't escape the feeling that everything will go on forever. I was caught by my reflection in the plate glass of the Beverly Hills Balloon Store. Smiling guys twisted balloons into animal shapes at ten bucks a throw. People were lining up. I certainly looked every inch a butler, solid, dependable, heavy-set. Unconsciously I straightened my tie.

When I got back Denver was hanging around the kitchen.

Rojay and the cherubs were busy being nice to him. Fong and the relatives muttered darkly.

'Hey, dude, let me give you a hand with that.' I was puffing a bit under my shopping bags. I don't know what I'd bought, but it didn't seem to make Fong any happier.

After he'd helped me Denver said, 'I've put something in your room.'

I said, guardedly, 'Is that chick still in there?'

Denver grinned, 'Sure. She's trying it on, as a matter of fact.'

Moments later we were in my apartment, looking at Lulu. Some of the feelings we had about it, I expect, were the same. Some were different. I said, 'Denver, there is a difference between a waitress and a French maid.'

Lulu posed voluptuously, 'I think it's cute.'

Denver said, 'I thought maybe she could wear rollerskates.'

Considering the outfit with Jayne Belle and her mother in mind, certainly rollerskates couldn't have made matters any worse. They might even enable Lulu to escape more easily when they spotted her. Conversely, there could be no escape for me.

'Where on earth did you get it?' was all I could think of saying. It was, as Lulu said, cute, in the worst possible way: the black skirt was shorter than the white frilly apron, which was pretty short. But it was the black fishnet stockings and matching satin bow which, against the flame of Lulu's locks, set every alarm bell ringing.

'Frederick's of Hollywood!' Denver's voice was husky with adolescent pride.

'Oh, God, Denver.' I tugged at my own bandbox hairstyle. 'We can't, we just can't.'

'Red Butler,' Denver came over to me with great earnestness and put both his hands on my shoulders. Every ounce of sincerity he could muster writhed on his face. 'I swear to you, I give you my *word* as a Jewish Hebrew and a graduate of Beverly Hills High that I will take *full responsibility* for this. There will be *no* comeback on you *whatsoever*.'

— 70 —

I looked over at Lulu, who smirked and stuck out her tongue. Something of my old self, the Public School Man, not a wretched servant, unafraid of the wrath of Jewish Princesses and Matrons, quivered deep in my psyche. Denver spotted it and pounced, 'Whaddya say, dude? It's too good to miss, isn't it?'

I nodded. It was.

The hot Los Angeles afternoon was cooling down. It was time to fetch the ladies from the beauty shop. I checked out the marquee before I left. Things looked much the same as they had done twenty-four hours before, only now there were more people. They were making lots of noise. Loudest by far was the group clustered round the imposing central figure of Julius Caesar.

Another figure, equally imposing, who would have been central if it had not been for the founder of the Julio Claudian dynasty, dominated the ranks of the living. He was spectacularly tall and powerful, with a powerful, beaky noise and penetrating eyes, high, flat cheekbones, the face of an Apache War Chief. His blue-black hair was long, pulled back fiercely from his brow into a ponytail tied with a leather thong. His muscular torso was startingly naked save for a sleeveless black leather jerkin. A huge golden sunburst on a long gold chain nestled in his luxuriant body hair. He wore tight black leather pants. In between nervous puffs on a Gauloise he spoke in a lisping falsetto: 'It's got to *go*, Boothby. I'm telling you for the *last time*.' Boothby looked rattled. 'He *is* Roman. I know not fifteenth century, but – '

'That's not the *point*, Boothby,' The world's Greatest Living Artist reached over to Boothby's scarf and tugged it gently. 'You just don't *understand* . . .'

Werner and Hoobey couldn't help letting their tense expressions soften into smugness. Boothby's discomfiture at the hands of his hero, his exposure to ridicule before other ranks, were hard not to welcome as balm to our base, servile souls.

Doctor Love arrived. He was looking tired and tense, his uniform crumpled. He was far from the insouciant boulevardier of Brooklyn. 'Hey, British,' he said, 'the man wants you in his office, *right now*.'

I walked to Kenny's office, rubbing vainly at my lapels and straightening my tie. What could be wrong? The list of possibilities was too long to explore fully on the journey. My mind was blank as I knocked.

'Come!'

'You rang, Sir?' I approached him across the thick pile. He had the full array of his lights on in the vast room. They blazed on the wealth of gold leaf with which every cornice and moulding was liberally coated. It was hard to make him out through the shimmering haze. Light flashed in his glasses as he lifted his head. I didn't like the look of it.

But his voice, when he spoke, was chummy. 'Come in, come in. Paul, I wanna ask you somethin'.'

'Yes, Sir?'

'You married?'

'Yes, Sir.'

'Never get married.'

'No?'

'No sir. It's a mistake.'

I cleared my throat and shuffled my feet. It seemed to me we were on stony ground. The glasses blazed at me penetratingly.

'You gotta mother-in-law?'

'Yes, Sir.'

'Does she dray you and gvetch you the whole goddam time?'

'I'm not sure if . . .'

'I wanna show you somethin'.'

We pushed past a bronze bust of Pompey the Great into his private bathroom. The place was full of scripts and financial reports. Kenny rested his hand on the shoulder of a garment hanging on a hanger as if it were an old friend. It was a black velvet jacket.

'Whadya think?'

'Very nice, Sir.' The lapels were, perhaps, a trifle wide.

'No objections to me wearing it?'

'It's hardly my place, Sir . . .' I found it best to stick strictly to my Jeeves script.

'Nothing in the book, I mean?'

'The book?'

'Book of rules. Etiquette.'

I shook my head in bewilderment.

'Iris says it's out of season.'

This time I scratched my head and looked at him blankly.

'Well' – Kenny's glasses flashed warningly – 'is it or isn't it? You're the guy supposed to have all the class.'

I drew myself up. 'There are no seasons, Sir, governing the wearing of velvet jackets, so far as I am aware.'

Kenny beamed. His glasses twinkled. 'That's good enough for me.'

The telephone on his desk rang. 'Shall I answer that, Sir?'

'Go ahead,' Kenny said absently, picking up a script. He had lost interest in me now.

I took up his phone. 'Graumann residence.'

'Where the *hell* are you?'

'Er . . . I'm with your husband . . .'

'Get down here right away – if you know what's good for you!'

Kenny said, 'Who is it?'

I put my hand over the receiver. 'It's your wife, Sir. She's at the beauty shop. She wants me to fetch her right away.'

'Tell her you're busy.'

I gripped the receiver more tightly and looked at him pleadingly.

He glared back.

I uncovered the mouthpiece and said tentatively, 'Hallo?'

'What the hell's the matter with you?'

'I'm afraid your husband says I'm busy.'

'Doing *what*, for Chrissakes?'

'Well, as a matter of fact,' (trying for the chatty, conversational note) 'we're casting our eye over his velvet jacket.'

'That horrible thing! It makes him look like a waiter. Tell 'im that. And *get down here*!' Jayne Belle hung up abruptly. I turned to Kenny, dropping the instrument onto its high-tech console with listless fingers. He seemed buried in a script.

'She does insist I go and fetch her, Sir.'

'Tell the chauffeur to go. That's what he's paid for. I need you here.'

I said, 'Yes, Sir,' and padded respectfully from the room.

— 4 —

Eight p.m. The place was lit up like Disneyland, inside and
out. Kenny and I had spent a testing twenty minutes fiddling
with dimmers, a favourite obsession of his. The twilight was
gleaming enough for the guests' cars to be showing lights.
They were pulling in now, thick and fast. Like all Beverly
Hills guests they were on parade dead on time. Consequently
the main body arrived all at once, like a sudden squall. They
left their cars wherever, often locked. The task of somehow
getting them parked fell to Doctor Love. The parapsychology
of soul was being tested to the limit: he hadn't been too happy
when I'd hoiked him out of the shower to go fetch the ladies,
and he was a good deal less so when he returned. Jayne Belle
had taken it out on him. His arrival rather than mine, at the
beauty shop, had inflamed her. It wasn't his fault but that
didn't help. He was under strict orders, as soon as his stint
as a valet parker was over, to change into a monkey suit and
help me help Rojay serve the multitude.

Kenny and I stood side by side in the entry hall, braced
to greet. He'd been dragooned into it by his wife, who still
had plenty to say both to him and to me, even after she'd
finished with Doctor Love. The jacket clung defiantly to his
puny frame. He sported a large matching bow-tie and loud
tartan trousers.

I wore my double-breasted jacket, modelled on Ralph
Richardson's in *Fallen Idol*. It gave me a certain presence on

occasions when there was 'company'. That evening it seemed to me to be less encrusted with foodstains and candlegrease than my other two jackets, which further recommended it. I had decapitated one of Iris's flowers, something big and bold, and stuck it in my buttonhole. Eyeing Kenny, I cautiously rubbed tired shoe leather up and down the backs of my striped trousers, just as the first revellers came barging over the moat and in through the open door.

We were engulfed in a gush of superlatives. The horde, so far all strangers to us, if not to each other, gaped and gesticulated wildly.

'Hi!' said Kenny, again and again.

'Good evening,' I said, bowing slightly from the waist. They shook our hands, both of us, both our hands, many not stopping short at kisses on the cheek. We kept smiling, pumping, clasping.

Someone, no stranger to me, loomed over the herd. It was Massimo di Los Angeles.

He shimmered before us. We gaped speechless, while two acolytes helped him out of a sable coat. He received it back from them, burying his face for a moment in its richness. He then dumped it, with the grand gesture of one who discards unwanted baggage, into Kenny's arms. The diminutive mogul all but disappeared. The great living artist turned to me and said, 'Mister Graumann. This is an *exquisite* pleasure.' He kissed both my hands. Before either of us had time to recover, the great man had passed on with his entourage. Several other guests dumped their superfluous belongings on Kenny.

The last of these wore a Philip Marlowe mac and brown slouch hat. He added the former to Kenny's pile, pressing it down enthusiastically until Kenny's inflamed features appeared above the surface. He put the hat on Kenny's head. 'Kennybaby! I always knew you'd make it to the coatcheck one day. Which way's the popcorn?' Under the mac the newcomer wore a brown striped suit, co-respondent shoes, and a loud painted tie with a diamond pin. He looked raffish, with thinning brown hair, an

Errol Flynn moustache, a leathery tan, and the generally sleazy air of a hood in a Fifties' B picture.

Kenny took it in good humour. 'Paul, I wantcha ta meet my ex-father-in-law, Sammy Peach. I hope ya remembered ta nail everything down. Now, *get me outa this*!'

I took the coats and my employer stumped off, exchanging banter with his wife's notorious father. They followed everyone else in the direction of the marquee. The hall was empty and I wandered about, wondering where to dump my burden. I heard a noise outside the ... d went to investigate.

... pillar, a big smile on ... nething that crackled ... d as big as a rolled ... to fill the universe.

... ke, Love . . .' My ... lly around.

Class Ticket type Adult Child OUT
STD CHEAPDY RTN CD ONE NIL
Date Number
30 SEP 93 94651 371605202003
Valid Price
AS ADVERTISED £3.20M
From
HORSHAM *
Route 1003
To
DORKING BR * DIRECT

British Rail

I don't want to lose my job.'
'You speak for you ownself.'
'Don't be silly, Love.'
'I had about all I cin stand o' these Jewish motherfuckers.'
'For God's sake . . . Please, please cool it.'
'Hey,' Love said, placing an arm around my rigid shoulders, 'I'm cool. How about you?'
I struggled. 'I'm just, you know . . .'
'A little uptight?'
I managed a pathetic grin. 'Just a little, perhaps.'
'Think maybe you should loosen up a little bit? Just one puff for yo ole brother Love?' Two brown fingers held temptation to my lips. I thought, what the hell. He was right. There was, there must be, a world beyond this.
I hadn't finished coughing when the sound of all the trouble I was in came floating through the door. 'What the *hell* are

all these coats doing on my floor? Where *is* everybody? Paul!'

Love took off. My arms made a few futile flaps. The moat gurgled mockingly. I knew Jayne Belle must be faced and headed off. I made for the door. We met on the threshold. Our eyes clashed in a moment of truth. Jayne Belle drew breath and her eyes narrowed. 'Paul?' I could feel guilt and confession wrestling their way in a stupid smile on my slack, trapped face. My lips moved to commence blurting . . .

Tyres crunched on the gravel behind me. A car door clunked. Jayne Belle's black eyes flickered momentarily away from my face.

'*Shop*!' It was the voice of Salvation. I spun round. 'Come along, Shaw. Let's have a bit of service.' Henry, Viscount Pelham, marvellous in full evening dress, sauntered across the drawbridge. 'Jayne Belle, darling . . .' I stood aside, not wishing to impede their embrace. 'However can you stand such a useless butler?'

'Henry!' Jayne Belle switched to her sugary voice. She had melted like a marshmallow. 'How sweet of you to come.'

'Can't rot on the beach forever.'

'Your evening clothes are just fabulous.'

'You don't look so bad yourself.' Jayne Belle's hourglass figure was tightly encased in something red and expensive. His Lordship patted her bottom.

'Henry!' She wriggled. 'Come along inside and let me show you . . . Paul, please park Lord Pelham's car.'

Henry turned to me, sniffed, winked. 'And mind my paintwork.'

Jayne Belle's voice faded back to me over the diminishing tap tap tap of her bustling stilettos. 'This guy's artwork is just *fabulous*, you must know his work, Massimo di Los Angeles. They say he's possibly the World's Greatest Living Artist . . .'

The World's possibly Greatest Living Artist was in full cry in the marquee. Taking five in Henry's Eldorado had given me the break I needed. I was further braced by a swift detour via my pantry and its boundless stock of strengthening restoratives. Even so, I was only just prepared for the setting in which our guest of honour was making his pitch.

Bright lights filled a polystyrene Greek temple in the centre of the tent. In the centre of the temple, standing on a plinth, declaiming with the rhetorical oratory of Ancient Times, was Massimo di Los Angeles. Grouped around him on smaller plinths, frozen in demure classical poses, cherubic boys made much of their anatomies.

'These will be my models. Michelangelo, my *Maitre* . . .' (Massimo simpered modestly. I caught Boothby whispering and nodding to Sammy Peach, as if in explanation. Sammy looked blank and restless) '. . . was preoccupied with male beauty. He was, at heart, a Greek. If he hadn't been forced to work for that horrid Pope . . .' (Massimo shrugged and spread his hands expressively) 'who knows? That is what we must explore here, in *our* Sistine Chapel, freed from the shackles of Christian convention.' Massimo leered over at Jayne Belle. I was standing behind her. She leaned across to Henry and hissed, 'I'm a closet Catholic at heart, honey.'

Massimo continued. 'Something definitely more pagan, more *contemporary* . . .' (a sigh escaped the gathered artlovers at the word contemporary) 'the ideal of an Earthly Paradise, sought by the Greeks, frowned on by Roman and Christian morality, what better setting have we than here,' (Massimo looked around, nodding at the nodding crowd) 'here, surely, in Beverly Hills, we have *found* Paradise on Earth, and hardly a Christian in sight.'

There was general clapping at this speech, and the odd 'Oyve!' I heard, 'I heard *that*!' from over by Rojay's buffet. Towering over the *cuisine Californienne*, his new-found partner's arm around his waist, Mustaffa the Leader was resplendent in full regalia and a larger, gold turban. He smiled a rapturous, reptilian smile. His slitted lizard eyes glowed yellow.

At this moment Doctor Love appeared. He, too, had spotted the Leader and was making his way towards him. He had changed out of his chauffeur's uniform, but not into the regulation monkey suit specified by Jayne Belle. The parapsychologist of soul looked much like his old self, from jaunty denim cap to new denim skating boots.

I followed his progress with fascination for some time over Jayne Belle's shoulder. How long could it be before she spotted him? She was fully absorbed, first by the gallantry of Henry, next by the striking up of Boothby Cunningham's string quartet.

Boothby had engaged these musicians, he had insisted on them despite the contribution to the evening promised by Denver and the Hot Hebrews. He thought them appropriate to the general ambience, whereas Denver and the Hot Hebrews he thought inappropriate in the extreme. He was, in fact, inconsolable on the subject, utterly unable to construe the connection between the Deadhead influence and the Renaissance. Jayne Belle, her maternal instincts for once aroused, had managed a compromise between conflicting artforms. Denver had been forced to promise that he would not go on before midnight. By then, it was secretly hoped, all the guests who mattered would have gone home.

But hardly a dozen bars of Vivaldi went by before the marquee was rocked to its guy ropes by a massive electronic *twang*. Denver, anticipating no less shrewdly than his blood kin, had lied. Greatly magnified by the water of the pool, the hideous cacophony that was the Hot Hebrews warming up, proved strong competition for one cello, two violins and a viola.

Reactions were mixed. Mustaffa and Doctor Love approved and said, 'Yeah!'

In front of me Henry Pelham turned and smiled.

Beside him Jayne Belle frowned darkly.

I turned myself, partly to avoid her eye, in the general direction of the outrage, to find Kenny standing beside me.

'Oh, hallo, Sir,' I said. His glasses were twinkling. He didn't answer.

Jayne Belle turned and faced us both. She said, 'Well, are you going to stand there and see me mortified in front of my guests?' It was hard to say at which one of us this was directed. I shuffled my feet and coughed, 'Erm . . .'

Henry said, 'Come along Crighton, jump to it!'

Jayne Belle's eyes were smouldering dangerously. 'This isn't a *joke!*'

'No, no, absolutely . . .'

'*Do* something!'

'Right!'

'Kenny, you asshole, are you going to let this happen to me? The most important night of my *life!*'

'He's your son.'

'I'm your *wife*, goddammit!'

Kenny looked up at me. 'You noticed?'

'What the *hell* are you talking about?' Jayne Belle's colour was mounting to match her dress.

'Arright arready! I'm going, I'm going.' I wished I was too. 'If I can be of any assistance, Sir . . .' I started to say. But Jayne Belle was onto me. 'You stay here, Paul. Lord Pelham needs more champagne.'

Wistfully, I watched the dayglo of Kenny's tartan trews as they made their getaway. I made my own to the zinc tub where numerous bottles were cooling. I managed a fizzy swig that almost choked me. I poured Henry's drink and an extra one, just in case, and prepared to blunder back, the long way round.

The twanging and screeching abruptly died. Kenny had achieved his goal. The quartet, a greyish group in dark blue tuxedos, who had laid their instruments aside with the resigned patience of Hollywood old-timers who have seen it all, resumed. More Vivaldi sliced the air.

I decided not to bother delivering Henry's drink but to get straight on with the important business of averting another crisis. I headed fast in the direction of the buffet.

Among the group around it were Mustaffa and Doctor Love. Squeezed up against Love was Tracey. She was looking upset. 'Go change!' she wheedled. 'If Mom sees you she'll let you go.'

I scanned the room. Kenny had returned and stood with one hand resting on a cold bicep of Julius Caesar, talking to Victor Ventura. There was something conspiratorial about the pair, as though the ides of March were come again. They kept casting smiling glances at the quartet.

The sudden crash of a single electric chord galvanised the gathering and sent the cellist's bow flying in the air. A pregnant pause of two beats, then Denver and the Hot Hebrews cut loose with 'Hava Nagila'.

The smiles of Kenny and the old movie star matured into laughs of Yiddisher glee as they both 'got down', their triple bypasses for the moment forgotten. They linked arms and their legs shot out like Cossacks. A clapping circle soon formed around them. Victor's denim cap slipped over one eye and Kenny's trews were shown to particular advantage.

Outside that circle another one, smaller and tighter, formed, of those not amused: Boothby Cunningham, Iris, Jayne Belle. I'd managed by a hair's breadth to avoid her eye when a new and even lower low broke out.

Egged on by assorted dissidents and waiters, Mustaffa, Werner and some mischievous cherubs, Doctor Love had reverted to his Brooklyn roots – and beyond – and was performing some wild and uninhibited rollerboogie. His long, graceful body pumped and flailed.

Worse still was his partner. Lulu appeared with a flourish, as if she had jumped out of a cake. As Denver had hoped, she was on wheels. They made her legs look longer and her skirt shorter and they tilted her arse. She looked good. She had worked out a vamping routine which went well with the Doctor's antics. She waved one apron-string like a tail and went, 'Ow ow ow ow ow.'

A crowd soon gathered to rival Kenny's. I noticed Henry

Pelham and Sammy Peach standing together like two sly old foxes sizing up a spring chicken. As they whispered together it was easier to guess at *their* conspiracy. Henry looked up and I caught his eye. Something flickered there for a moment before he raised a finger and a fist in a characteristically obscene gesture.

Someone else near me was watching with very different reactions, but for the same reasons. Tracey, like her mom, was not amused. Doctor Love's reaction to Lulu was making her mad as hell. She had the same black eyes as her mom's, like the tips of pistol-barrels. They were boring into Love, the colour on her downy teenage cheeks livid.

Love cupped his hands behind Lulu's neck and spun her round. She lost her footing. He caught her, moving one hand down to the small of her back. She hung there, her face upturned to his. The Doctor stooped, his eyes fixed on hers. We all held our breath.

'You bastard!' Tracey was on him, her small fists windmilling, pounding. Love fell back, laughing and tumbling into the crowd. They held him up, but his wheels were revving out of control. He tried to fend off Tracey, laughing with disbelief.

'Hey, sweetheart, slow down. Wassamatter wi' you?'

'You *fucking asshole*!' Tracey's voice rose about five octaves above pitch. 'You think you can screw me and then fuck around with this . . . this . . . in my own *house*?'

This speech silenced not only Love, but the whole marquee. Love looked from side to side and made play down motions with his hands. But the damage was done. Jayne Belle broke violently into the circle, pushed her daughter out of the way and stood in front of Love, hands on hips, breathing hard. I thought she was going to start in punching where Tracey left off, but in the end she was just coherent enough to say:

'You're *fired*!'

The Hot Hebrews had ground to a temporary halt but now mercifully started another number. Love's reply was drowned in it. He slunk off. Tracey tried to follow him, but Jayne Belle had her by the wrist. She screamed into her tearstained face. Over the din I caught the word '. . . schwartzer . . .!'

'Bloody yids.' I looked up shocked to find Henry at my side.

'For God's sake, Henry!' Things were bad enough.

'They're the worst racists of the lot, you know.'

'All the same.'

Henry changed tack. 'Enough bloody arse bandits here to satisfy the whole of Eton College. Those JAPs are all bloody fag hags. I don't know how Kenny stands it.'

'Henry. I do have to work here, you know.'

'That bit of ginger pussy, though.' Henry set his jaw and ground one fist into his palm. 'I'd like to bend *her* over and drive her home.'

I said, 'Why don't you?' Thinking of the Eldorado and Lulu's known tastes.

'Too late, old boy.'

'How d'you mean?'

'Sammy Peach. In like Flynn. Look.' Henry nodded in the direction of the pool. Two figures were disappearing into the darkness.

'Good Lord! How does he do it?'

Henry said, 'Aha,' and laid one finger along the side of his nose.

I stood by the front door, aching for the last guests to leave. It was after midnight. In the next three hours all traces of the party must be cleared away. That was Jayne Belle's rule. It was hard work and Rojay's cherubs were sulky. They wanted to go to bed, to get it on, to make it out to the beach, to be in the movies. They chattered eagerly, about auditions, agents, friends with scripts, of a world beyond waitering to be lived, surely, one day, one day soon, in the houses where for now they worked and watched and envied.

Mustaffa and Rojay were long gone. There was no sign

of Doctor Love. When the last item of partyware had been cleared, washed, polished, stored away and accounted for, the last flower arrangement appropriated, the last cherub safely off the premises ('*Ciao*, hun, see you next time') I went in search of him.

The chauffeur lived, not surprisingly, over the garage. There was a downstairs door, an inside staircase, a small, cheaply comfortable pad with a shower and a view of the 'area'. The downstairs door was open. I stopped at the bottom of the stairs.

'Love? Are you up there?' I whispered.

We mostly talked in whispers, the help and the kids. We were all infected with a paranoid sense of conspiracy, of being overheard, caught in the act. Jayne Belle was never far away, round every corner, up every stairwell, behind every rood-screen. There were telephone intercom sets everywhere, with speakers which squawked like darning needles in your ear any hour of the day or night. There was one by my bed. I never knew when it might go off. They had little speakers which could so easily be listening devices, feeding information about us night and day to some secret, central computer.

I crept up a few steps. 'Love!' a little louder, but still a whisper. I had decided that if he was asleep I would wake him.

Silence. I crept on up. At the top I could see light flickering through the doorway of the room. I padded softly in. The big wooden colour TV was on, the volume turned right down. A game show. Love was passed out on the grey settee, his legs splayed out before him onto the orange rug. His skates were still on. His mouth was open, his ears plugged by the headset of his walkman.

'Hey, Love,' I shook him gently by the shoulder. He stirred, opened his eyes, blinked, shook his head, turned to look at me.

'Paul. Whass happ'n'n?'

'You fell asleep.'

Love scrutinised his imitation Rolex. 'Man! It's four o'clock!'

'You can't sleep here like this.'

'Man, I *was* sleepin' here like this. Hav'n a real groovy dream, too.'

'I'm sorry.'

'Oh, don't apologise. I was only gettin' a body rub from that Lulu chick, is all.'

'And did you dream you got fired?'

Love sat up. 'Man, was that only a dream?'

'I'm afraid not.'

'Ooee. For a moment there you had me worried.'

'You mean you don't mind?'

'*Mind*? Man, I gotta get outa here!'

'What about Tracey?'

'Tracey!' Love started ticking off his fingers, 'is jailbait. She gotta mouth. She gotta mother. She gotta Gran'ma . . . man, I'm *outa* here. *Fast!*'

'I thought you loved her.'

'I love *you* brother. Don't you know that?'

I hunkered down, kneading my hands, embarrassed. 'Well . . .' I looked up. 'I love you too, Love.'

'You cin handle it you ownself now, I reckon.'

'You think so?'

'You a real class butler act now. They can't ever find another one like you. You got them motherfuckers by the balls. If you only knew it.'

'You think so? I thought I was about to get fired.'

'*Fired? Bullshit!* Next time they start shittin' on you, you take it from the Doctor. You gonna ax them bastards for a *raise*.'

'A *raise*! Don't be crazy!'

'Listen to me, British. I'm outa here. I'm jess a no account nigger. You cin get folks like me outa the *trees*. They know that. But *you*, you got *class*. You got much more class than they do. You got *everything* they want and know they can't never get. You got centuries of *style*.'

It was food for thought. 'You really think so?'

'You better believe it. You jess gotta *trade* on it. Promise me you will.'

'Well, I . . .'

'Go on, British. Your jolly old word of honour to the Doctor.' Love held up his palm. Awkwardly I slapped it. He gripped my fingers, looked deep into my eyes. 'We'll meet again, bro.'

'I hope so. Where will you be?' Suddenly my voice was hollow with the shock of parting. Love grinned. His teeth shone white like the Ivory Coast. 'Who knows? Jess stay on the Soul Train.'

Suddenly we both started laughing. I said, 'You'll probably be the conductor.'

— 5 —

Later that morning, about four hours later, I got the call.

'Come up!'

I hadn't really slept. I looked in the mirror and passed a hand across my blotchy face. Apprehension and residual stimulants surged painfully in my bosom. Jayne Belle had summoned me in her death-lizard voice, Tyrannosaurus Regina.

'Come up' meant the boudoir. On reluctant feet I plodded up the thickly carpeted stairs and knocked as confidently as I could before pushing the buttons on her security lock.

'Come!'

They didn't work. I called lamely through the wood, 'Is it still 2-2-3?'

'I changed it.' The word 'changed' and the wrenching open of the door in my face were simultaneous and forceful. 'You know why?'

I took a startled step back. 'Er . . .'

'Because that horrible harlot was in the house!' Her eyes blazed and her substantial bosom, restricted only by a towelling robe, heaved.

'I look awful, I know,' she added.

'No, no . . .'

'Stop staring at me!'

I glanced over her shoulder, the only alternative view. Her mother was slumped in an armchair, clad in a grey sweatsuit, looking generally grey.

'She might've stolen anything!' Jayne Belle reverted to the business in hand.

'She did.' Iris's face was a mask of gloom. 'She stole my husband.'

'This is *your* fault, Paul.' Jayne Belle fuelled the blaze with reproach.

'I don't quite see . . .' It wasn't much of a defence but it inspired Jayne Belle to redouble her attack. 'Do you deny that you hired that girl?'

'Well, I . . .'

'Denver says you did.'

'He did?' His treachery shocked but failed really to surprise me.

'Look at Mumsy.' We both did. Her face was squished like a lemon. Jayne Belle turned back to me. 'She's very upset. How could you?'

Iris raised her morose mask to me. 'I thought we were friends.'

'Of course we are.' I made a huge effort to get off the defensive with a surge of gallantry.

'Mumsy and I have been discussing your future.' My heart sank. Love's fine words about raises seemed to belong to another, braver world.

Jayne Belle moved further into the room. 'Come in.' She curled up in another armchair, her head resting against a heart-shaped pillow which read: *Living Well is the Best Revenge*, and regarded me in a nestling, speculative sort of way. I remained standing, my hands behind my back, like Prince Charles, but not quite.

'I oughta fire your ass outa here!' I lowered my head, almost in acquiescence, guilty as charged, thinking of Natasha. How awful if her prediction turned out to be correct.

'But my mother thinks we should give you one more chance.' I looked up with the requisite look of gratitude and hope.

'Which, considering what you did to her . . .'

I bowed low. 'The quality of Mercy is not strained . . .'

'. . . and all the experience she's got of domestics . . .' The word stung as it was meant to.

'You're never gonna make a great flower-arranger, let's face it.'

I grinned hideously. 'I guess not.'

'And your napkin-folding *stinks*.'

The grin became a snort of self-depreciation. I looked at Iris. She shook her head.

'All domestics need *certain skills*,' Jayne Belle was blazing away at me again, 'not just some goddam superfatted accent!' There was a pregnant hush in the room as we all paused to reflect on this.

Jayne Belle broke it, like glass. 'Mother thinks we might make a gourmet chef out of you.'

Caught off guard I blurted, 'But we already have a chef!'

'There's nothing *gourmet* about Fong,' Iris pointed out sourly. 'We need someone who can appreciate the finer things . . .'

'Who can respond to the training sensitively,' said Jayne Belle.

'The training?'

'Rojay is opening the most fabulous cooking school. I'm backing him. He's *so* talented.'

Rojay's academy of *cuisine Californienne* was way down on La Brea, south of Santa Monica. My fabulously expensive lessons at least got me out of the house. On my way to the first one, I hung a detour through Beverly Hills and went to my bank, First Oil Charter, on Rodeo. The valet took my Mercedes and the smiling but well-armed commissionaire greeted me. I waited briefly in the short, roped-off line. Security guards loafed casually at strategic corners. Everything was very muted and discreet. A muzac tape whispered an airconditioned medley of Eagles tunes. An elderly, uniformed greeter chattered inanely to the waiting customers. Both banking and working at First Oil Charter, he repeated, gave added meaning to the old-fashioned serenity of American life. Sun poured reliably through hessian-draped plate glass.

Number 8 lit up and an electronic bell chimed softly. I had by a hair's breadth missed the demure Japanese girl with blood-red mouth and tailored beige outfit. My guy was called Hratch Durdurian.

'How may I help you today, sir?'

'I'd like to check my balance, please.'

'May I have your account number and some ID?' He looked suspicious and I felt, as I always did, like a scheming but transparently naive con-man. As nonchalantly as I could, I passed my cheque book through the armoured glass.

'Sir, do you have anything to back this up? Credit cards?'

'The one I asked you for hasn't come through yet.' This confirmed his worst fears. He picked up a telephone, watching me carefully all the time. He talked softly for a while, then passed me a slip of paper.

'I have to ask you to write your mother's maiden name on there, Sir.'

I sighed grumpily, wrote it and passed it through. He scrutinised it, looking at his computer screen. The rest of First Oil Charter transacted serenely on.

Hratch looked down and up, frowned. I could see the disappointment. He wrote something on the back of the same slip, passed it through. It seemed an outrage for someone with a credit balance of almost two thousand dollars to be treated so. Hratch was less impressed than me. Two grand is not a lot of money at First Oil Charter.

'I'd like to wire this to my wife's account in London.'

Hratch Dudurian looked doubtfully at his watch, shook his head. 'Won't go now till morning.'

'But can I do the wire now? I've done it before at this time.'

Hratch looked at me. His eyes were blank. 'See the wire clerk.'

I got outside after sitting through more courteous third degree at the wire clerk's desk, to find I'd forgotten to get my parking ticket validated.

'Shit. I don't have time to go back now.' I eyed the valet. He sized up my butler's uniform. We were both members of the same sub-stratum.

'That'll be five bucks today, buddy.'

It gets residential and confusing around that part of La Brea, in the high five thousands, the low-rent district Rojay had chosen to base his high-price cuisinery. I had to hang some Us and was late, not nearly as unruffled as a butler ought to be.

The school was in a bungalow with a long, wide, concrete driveway and a concrete yard out back. The concrete was covered with cars. I squeezed mine in near the gate. There were Cadillacs, personalised sunshine state number plates, a white Rolls Corniche. A sticker on its back bumper read, *Life's a Beach*.

I walked in through the open front door. The place was all space, polished wood floor, plants, sunny white walls. Another open door led through to where I could hear the buzz of voices.

Apart from Rojay and the odd cherub I was confronted by a solid wall of women. The air in the room was tangy with their expensive fragrances. Every eye, many quite jaded, turned on me as I clumped to a halt on the hollow peg and groove in the doorway. The buzz faltered. Rojay looked up.

'Maybe we can get started now.'

'Sorry, Rojay. Unavoidably detained.'

'My God! Is that accent for real?'

'You gotta cousin?' The ladies seemed pleased with me. I glanced around, smiling, trying to take them in singly rather than as a blur. The effort made me slightly queasy.

Rojay said, 'He can't boil an egg.'

One of them, a brunette in tightly tailored denim with plenty of jewellery, said, 'He shouldn't have to,' giving me a big red smile.

'OK girls,' Rojay said, pulling on a high chef's hat, 'cut the crap. Let's boogie. Find a partner and pick a booth.' The walls were divided into small wooden stalls, each containing cooking-tackle: work surface, chopping board, blender, peppermill, lethal looking knives, and so on. My heart sank as the group paired up. They all seemed so familiar with everything, including each other. Making the advance to any one of them was impossible. I stood rooted, like a wallflower at dancing class.

All down the wall where Rojay stood, behind a long wooden table, was a bank of high-tech aluminium ovens and burners. Beyond these, in the farthest corner, angled in slanting shadow, somehow out of the mainstream, was a booth. It attracted me. It had the strong pull of the back row of class, where the liggers and dunces hang out. I started across. I figured if I collared a booth I might draw a partner, or, better still, might not.

Halfway over I was pulled up, floundering, right out in the open. Someone else was going for my booth, almost there, ahead of me. If I got there after she did no one would believe it was the booth I was after. Fatally I hesitated, mind seized, gaping about. Everywhere seemed full. I held up my hands and gawked at Rojay. He took me in, slowly shook his head, looked around for me, his eye fetching up finally in the corner.

'Hey, Suzanne, sweetheart, is anyone sharing with you?'

'Not yet anyway.' A high, playful, Southern whine.

'You got it.' Rojay indicated me over with a flourish.

I planted a smile on my face and waded in. At least I couldn't be said to be hitting on her. The decision hadn't been mine. No one knew my thoughts. It was a gift, in a way. My heart thumped. It wasn't going to be easy to concentrate on cooking.

'Hi.' I hove to.

She was busy dismantling the blender. She looked up, 'Hi,'

looked straight down again, came up moments later with the blade, looked at me, this time full on. 'I'm Suzanne, by the way.'

'I'm Paul.' I held out my hand. She put the blade down and took it, but carefully, as if it were something else that might be cooked, or useful. She was tall. In sneakers she was tall as me, seemed taller because of her willowiness. Her honey hair was long, wispy at the ends, glowing with clean health. She had slavic cheeks, grey almond eyes. Her nose was too long, and pointed. She wore tomboy clothes, faded denim jacket and jeans. The jeans were tight, with a boy's fly. Under the jacket she wore a bright white T-shirt, very plain. Her breasts moved freely beneath the fabric. She was young, much younger than the room average, no more than twenty-five. In her ears and on her fingers she wore tiny jewels, complicating the tomboy. Around one wrist, on a black, leather strap, she wore a tiny expensive watch.

'What on earth are you doing in a place like this?' I couldn't help saying.

'A nice girl like me?'

Her faked archness put me more at ease. Bolder, I said, 'Are you a nice girl?'

She dropped the act and went back to the blender. 'That's for you to find out, honey.' She kept her eyes down for a few moments while I floundered. 'If you're lucky.'

'I, er, have to come here. For my job.'

'Sure,' she said briskly. 'You're a domestic.'

I knew I had to fight back. 'And what are you?'

She cocked her head at me, pursed her lips. Her mouth was small, but full, like a flower, the petals wrinkled. She flapped a hand. 'Oh, I'm just a gal, you know. Kinda bored.'

'It still seems an odd choice of – '

'Look, I just want to learn to cook, OK?' Little bright spots appeared on her cheeks.

We both fiddled around in silence with the blender and its blades, while Rojay bustled around the room, distributing sheets

with the recipe of the day. 'When you're done I make you eat it.'
He got to us. 'Everything OK?'

'Sure,' I said.

Suzanne said, 'I guess so.'

We looked at our sheets. I looked up, caught her eye unexpectedly. She looked wary, surprisingly insecure. 'Everybody
knows southern belles can't cook.'

I smiled, shook my head, looked down at my sheet. 'God
knows how we're going to cook this.'

'We'll be fine. Don't you think so?'

I looked up. She seemed to be asking me something, playing
with a button on her jacket. Surprised, I said, 'Sure, Suzanne,
of course we will.'

'That's all right then. C'mon. Let's get to work.'

We made gnocchi and an upside-down torte. Rojay was as
good as his word and made us eat it. Wine was provided to
wash it down and the class soon turned into a party. The
girl-talk raged outrageously about me as if, in my uniform, I
was invisible. *Pas devant les domestiques* meant nothing here,
apparently. Rojay bitched with the best of them. I would
have felt completely out of it, if it hadn't been for Suzanne.
With her urchin air she too seemed like an onlooker at the
feast. She became increasingly brattish as the wine went down.
The spots of colour reappeared. She sloshed more into our
glasses.

'Having fun, old boy?'

'Absolutely.'

'Drink up.'

'Well, I . . .'

'C'mon.'

'Duty calls, I'm afraid.'

'All the best butlers drink, I thought.'

'Not necessarily in the afternoon. They can smell it.'

'I thought we might go get a cocktail after this.'

'I've got to get back to work, I'm afraid.'

'You're a little uptight, aren't you?'

'I just don't want to lose my job.'

The party broke up. Next week we would prepare lobster with sauce Americaine. The ladies couldn't wait.

I followed Suzanne into the glittering sunshine. Everyone was clambering into their cars, shrieking farewells. I thought I'd better get mine out of the way. I wanted to say something lasting to her before we parted but she sauntered on, slightly out of reach. When she got to the white Rolls she took the key out of her breast pocket and turned, posing against the door. 'Y'all *sure* you won't change your mind?'

Driving back along the flat streets, the sunlight filtering through the palms, I reflected emptily on the recent past. Common sense and duty had prevailed. How many men could, like me, have refused? But was it a triumph of will or a cop-out? I knew what Suzanne thought, and my manhood quailed. Smug self-congratulation wasn't working. The low that they say succeeds every high was setting in. The dark gates of Chateau Graumann hove into view. I pressed my beeper. They swung open. I drove slowly through. In my mind I could hear them clanging shut behind me, shutting out the world of white cars and cocktails, possibly forever.

A few days later I thought I'd better call Natasha. I could check that she had received the money and affirm that I was, after all, still gainfully employed.

I set my Dreambar snooze alarm to wake me with KLOS soft rock at 6 a.m. It would be 10 p.m. in Sussex. Natasha should still be up.

Dialling in the grey light, my morning mouth cloyed with toothpaste, I felt sick. The roof of my mouth became dryer and dryer as the English ringing tone droned on. I was on the point of giving up, relieved in a way to opt for the comfortable monotony of my day and be spared the pain of distant emotions, when the ringing stopped and a cracked voice said, 'Hallo?' I recognised it as Millie, an ancient railway widow who 'did' for my mother-in-law in exchange for a cot in an attic and the odd scrap of food.

'Hallo,' I said, 'Millie?'

'Is that you, Nigel?'

'No, it isn't Nigel. It's Paul. How are you?'

'I thought it couldn't be Nigel.'

'I want to speak to Natasha, Millie.'

'He was here only a little while ago, you see.'

'Is Natasha there, Millie? I want to speak to her. These calls are a bit expensive.'

'That's what I'm just tellin' you. He picked 'er up a while ago. In 'is car.'

'Picked her up?'

'Nigel did. In that swishy car. Off to dinner, they was. She did look lovely, Miss Natasha did.'

'When d'you think they'll be back?' The transatlantic echo threw my voice back at me, bleak and shrill. Behind my dry mouth my throat was closing up.

'Oh, I couldn't say, dear. Very late they is, sometimes.'

I stared out at the pool. Early steam was rising. The sun was still a disc behind the smog, beyond the dusty palms. I felt heavy staring out, sitting on the edge of my bed, my face slack, my chest tight.

The intercom squawked and jerked me back.

'Honey, are you there?'

'Good morning!' I bellowed heartily.

'How are you today?' Jayne Belle's voice was comfortingly warm and caressing.

'Extremely well. How are you?'

'Oh, I'm OK. I'm so glad you're happy. Are you happy?'

'Absolutely!'

'I'm glad. Do you love being my butler?'

'You know I do.'

'Really? Love?'

'Love.'

'My husband has five for breakfast in his office. Can you do it?'

'Of course! When?'

'In about five minutes.'

On my way to cooking school the following week, the car planed dreamily down the mellow boulevards. I felt good. It was a nice day. Going south on La Brea I felt some excitement nipping at my throat. Would we be partnered the same way as last time? My excitement grew into mild anxiety. By the time I was parked and strolling nonchalantly through the door it had matured into full-blooded panic.

I searched the room. A blur of bangled suntans greeted me. 'Hi!' We were all great friends this week, seasoned muckers in the same platoon, no longer inhibited by novelty.

As I moved with subdued haste to my corner, our corner, Rojay slung an intimate arm around my shoulders. 'Hi, babe. All set?'

'Sure.' I glanced around the cubicle, looking for a bag or something. There was just a plain sheet of paper on a worktop: today's recipes.

'Did you put that there?' I spoke casually to Rojay, my eyes working the room.

Rojay glanced down. 'You got a problem with lobster?'

'No, it's not that, I just . . .'

This time Rojay searched the room as well. He squeezed my neck in the crook of his arm and breathed hard in my ear. 'Forget it, baby.'

'I don't follow you, Rojay.'

'You want pussy, forget that one.'

'Oh? Why's that?'

'Trouble, baby, with a capital T.'

For the first hour it still seemed possible she might show up.

We dropped living lobsters into boiling water. We reserved their flesh. We crushed their shells into pans with butter and wine to produce the necessary juices for our *sauce Americaine*. Some of the ladies squeaked with alarm, would *never* eat lobster again. It was all so *pagan*. It was, but the little god Pan in me was on a different track, thinking about Suzanne. He wouldn't give up, despite my telling myself that after nearly two hours it was nonsense. Anyway, I had no interest in Suzanne. She was fun, sure, but so what? And as Rojay said, she was very probably trouble. For some poor guy, but certainly not for me. Pan finally convinced me that a girl like that, wild and troublesome, would probably turn up at the end of the class just for the party. That was the sort of girl she was. I was at last able to attack the task before me with real commitment, adding an over-generous dose of cognac to my *sauce Americaine*. When Rojay showed me how to caramelise a fig, I was passionately receptive.

But the party went ahead without Suzanne. The ladies gobbled it up, the bestiality of the pot quickly forgotten. The sauce was fabulous, the figs divine. I amused and entertained the class, the butler as court jester, my despondency transfigured into a wild and spurious gallantry by the icy bottle of rosé d'Anjou meant for sharing with Suzanne.

Driving home with my heart in my mouth, adrenalin battling the alcohol in my blood, haunted eye on the mirror for cops, wet hands gripping the wheel, my soul was imploring the Mercedes not to weave. LA streets are wide and all-too easy to weave over. The seductive laidbackness, the monotonous gleaming glide, can for the unwary become an irreversible slide to jail after a demanding and dehumanising roadside examination. Lights change, cops appear. Life can change with terrifying suddenness in LA.

I made it through the armoury of our security gates – glad of their impenetrability today – parked the car with a flourish, oozing relief from every pore, and fingered my way through the digital lock on the kitchen door. My intention was to win through unnoticed to my room for a cup of tea and a sobering snooze.

I started the sneak across the tiled back-pantry floor and was within kissing distance of my goal when the unwelcome voice of Fong stopped me in my tracks.

'Missee call you. Vey *angly*.'

'Oh, God. When?'

'Ayee donno. Lottsa times.'

'What she say?' Being British I spoke pidgin English to Fong, which I hoped seemed chummy and not patronising. His inscrutable indifference made it hard to know.

'She say, "where my fucking butler".' Fong paused to chop furiously at a chicken wing with his cleaver. 'Vey bad boy.'

I buzzed around on the intercom and tracked Jayne Belle down to the music room. Keeping my voice clear as a bell I hit her with the good news.

'Hi! I'm home!'

'Hi.' She made the word sound like a mudslide. 'Where the hella you been?'

'Cooking school. It was great. We learnt how to – '

'Come in here, will you?'

'Absolutely!'

I stared at my face in the mirror, stuck out my tongue. Fong kept on chopping. I thought I looked pink but passable. I tried to smell myself but couldn't be sure, so, straightening my tie, I gave myself a last, courageous look, thought of Agincourt, squared my shoulders, and sallied forth.

I was going well through the kitchen door when I crashed into Denver.

'Hey, Dude!' Denver beamed with youth as I tried to reassemble myself against the doorframe.

'Oho, brother, you look *wasted*!' Denver beamed some more.

'Bollocks! Wasted, what do you mean?'

'Man, you know what I'm talkin' about. You stink like a liquor store.'

'God, Denver, don't say that!'

Fong said, 'Ayee, vey bad boy!'

'I just had some wine at cooking school. It doesn't really notice, does it? I'm on my way to see your mom.'

'Oh, brother,' Denver's beam broadened, 'what wouldn't I give not to be you.'

'I heard that.'

'Just keep your distance, is all.'

The music room was a Louis-Quinze affair with plenty of ormolu and scrollwork and paintings of the French 'decorative' school. Confronted by the gilded panels of its closed double doors I knocked with what I hoped was a nice blend of resolution and discretion.

'Come!' Jayne Belle's voice came clear as cut crystal through the woodwork. Inside, the one concession to music was a Steinway grand of phenomenal value, with the lid open. I stationed myself carefully alongside the instrument, keeping it between us, observing Jayne Belle warily across the expanse of hand-tooled wood and wire. It gave off a pleasing, musty aroma.

Jayne Belle had been working out some of her anger in the gym. She sat in her grey sweatshirt on a low blue chair with golden legs. The glass-top table before her was littered with mail-order catalogues. When the going gets tough, the tough go shopping. Yellow markers hung like hungry tongues out of the glossy pages.

Black eyes bored out of a putty face into my glowing pinkness. I breathed as shallowly as I could.

'Where the *hell* have you been?'

'I told you, cooking school.'

'I needed you *here*.'

'I'm sorry.' It was a relief to hang my head.

'Can you cook yet?'

'Well, I – '

'My husband thinks it's time we put you to the test.'

'But I've only had two lessons.'

'They last long enough, goddammit!'

'There's a lot of basic technique to be grasped first.'

'Well grasp this. My husband has some very important people coming to dinner Thursday. That's Fong's night off.'

'That's tomorrow!'

'That's right. There's only two of them, for Chrissakes. It's not as if we're asking the whole fucking world. Can't I have company in my own house if I want to? Do I have to ask your permission?'

'No, no. Of course you can. Absolutely!'

'And make sure it's fabulous. My husband needs to impress this guy.'

Taking this as my exit line I headed for the door, looking as much like a man with menus on his mind as I could. I had almost made it when she said. 'Take these with you, will you, honey?' in her cooing, turtle-dove voice. She was gathering up the catalogues. She looked up, smiling, as I bent low over her to receive my burden, my eyes fixed on her eyes. The package passed from her hands to mine. I straightened, turned, got back to the door, turned again. She was still smiling.

I decided to go for the lobsters. At Ecole Rojay the dish had seemed simple enough. Kenny had a meeting in his office all afternoon and because it was Fong's day off I couldn't go out. I was on standby with my silver tray of low-cal high-fibre refreshments until well after five. I made a frantic phone call to Phil's. They would deliver the lobsters before six-thirty. No, they would not forget. No, they did not sell figs. I wasn't sure I could handle caramelising after *sauce Americaine*. It was to this dish that I was nailing my colours. Depending on its outcome I would either be ahead of or out of the game when dessert time came around. I checked the freezer for ice-cream. Thirty-two varieties set my mind at rest.

I was pleased and surprised to find I had retained the recipe sheet. I spread it out like a prayer on the kitchen table. In between the demands of my clientele in Kenny's office, I hurried from place to place, assembling ingredients. Arranging them before me – cream, butter, brandy, herbs, a nice cold bottle of Chardonnay – made me feel confident, even competent, almost cordon bleu. I closed the front door on the last of Kenny's guests and hurried to the back door where the bell was ringing. It was the lobsters.

I had ordered six to be on the safe side. They were in a large cold cardboard box, which the minion from Phil's set on the table. Scrabbling noises issued alarmingly from the box. It manoeuvred ouija-like over the pine surface. One corner lifted and a claw poked out.

I started back just as Denver entered the room.

'Wha's happ'nin', Dude?' said Denver, looking at the box. It had just knocked over the brandy bottle. I picked it up.

'Starting a little early, aren't you, Red?' He took the bottle from me and pulled the cork.

'So would you if you had to deal with *that*.'

Denver absently digested a couple of swallows of five-star Remy Martin and flipped over the lid of the box, peering in. He quickly jerked upright.

'Oh, man, that is *gross*!'

'Denver,' I took a mouthful of Remy myself, 'somehow or other I have to get them into the pot.'

'No way.'

'We're talking about tonight's dinner.'

'No way. I'm off to Carnie's for a double chilli cheese.'

'I think I'm going to need your help.' My smile was spreading with the Remy Martin glow.

Denver held up his hands and started walking backwards. 'Oh, no. Believe me, buddy, there is no way that I am going to help you with *that*. They're not even dead.'

'Denver, we are talking job security here.'

'I don't care.'

'I'll play your tape at dinner if you help me.'

This stopped Denver. He wiped the heel of his hand thoughtfully over the neck of the bottle.

'Swear to God. The guy coming tonight is a *serious* bigshot.'

'In the music business?'

I shrugged. 'Who knows?'

'Might one enquire who the important person is tonight, Sir?'

Kenny Graumann and I were clambering about together in the confined space of the wine cellar. Not that the cellar was small. The quantity of wine stored in it was so large, the system of ladders and labels so complex, that two bodies in search of the same thing, the one big and butlerine, the other compact and impatient, could all too easily rub each other up the wrong way. Diplomatically unctuous banter, I found, sometimes eased the strain, although the cold roar from the megapowered temperature-control system was hard to compete with.

'What was that?'

'This fellow tonight, Sir.'

'What about him?'

'If we're looking for the Grand Echezaux it struck me he must be pretty important.'

'He's someone of Sammy's, if you wanna know.'

'Ah,' I said.

'Sammy's gotta project he wants me to . . . er, ah, mmm . . . he can't be here, ya know what I'm sayin?'

'Of course, Sir.'

'No need to say too much about this in front of Mrs Graumann.'

'No, Sir.'

'No point aggravatin' her.'

'Of course not, Sir.'

'Or her mother.'

'Or her mother.'

'Domingo somethin' or other. Sammy calls him Domingo Bananas.'

'He's South American?'

'Wants to put money in the movies.'

'That's good then, isn't it?'

'Lottsa money.'

'Did you want the '54 Echezaux, Sir?'

'Not *that much*.'

Denver and I had somehow wrestled the lobsters into the pot and I had left him in charge while I went to set the table. I had been only halfway through this when Kenny summoned me to the wine cellar. By the time I got back up it was after seven. Domingo Bananas and his partner were due at seven-thirty. As I hurried into the kitchen the beginning of a panic was forming behind the small cloud of Remy Martin in my brain. Denver had overcome his fear of lobsters enough to have eaten one, helped down by most of the bottle of Pinot Noir.

'Hey!' I said.

'Red!' He raised a congenial hand. 'This stuff is groovy.'

'I haven't even made the sauce yet.'

'Something else you've forgotten.' Denver's desire to help me glowed over his face. The old familiar vice clamped my chest.

'What?' I croaked.

'What are you going to give them for a starter?'

Down in the basement, behind a dingy doorway, an atmosphere of Chinese cooking pervaded Fong's lair. I staggered along a dark passage towards a chink of light, praying he was home, calling his name, all dignity of my high office utterly abandoned.

I burst into the room. 'Fong!' I cried, then halted, my mouth hanging open at what confronted me.

A line of Chinamen snaked around the yellow walls of the dingy room, shuffling slowly forward. The tail disappeared out of an opposite door. The first in line stooped over a wooden table to my right. Behind the table sat Fong, habitual ciggy smouldering on his blue lip. He frowned through the smoke, counting crumpled dollars into a tin box, entering them in a book. He turned narrow eyes on me, not all that welcoming. I felt a strong sense of having stumbled into a story by Sir Arthur Conan Doyle. The overpowering smell, if not of opium exactly, was certainly Chinese cooking of a very high order. A pot simmered sinisterly in one dark corner, tended by a subdued female whom I recognised as one of Fong's innumerable relations.

'Oh, I say, Fong, I'm awfully sorry. Hope I'm not interrupting anything.'

I glanced apologetically around the huddled line.

'*Vey* bizz.'

'It's just I . . . you know we've got these guests . . .'

Fong shook his head vigorously, shooting a stream of ash over his account book. 'No me helpee you. Nigh *off*!'

'No, no, no. Absolutely. It's just I wondered if you had any ideas about a starter. I'm afraid I've forgotten to do one.'

'Vey bad boy. No good.' Fong looked round the room, presenting me with his outstretched arm, like a ringmaster. The horde nodded appreciatively.

'Number One . . .' A titter passed among them.

Fong shook his head. 'Ayee. Number Nine!' The titter became a real laugh.

I laughed with the best of them. 'Like a *dog*!' That got them. The room was really roaring now. Even the subdued female by the stove was gulping and shrieking like a good'un.

Fong bared his teeth at me, obviously pleased at the popular response. 'What time eat?'

I glanced at my watch and felt myself whiten. 'In about a minute.'

The woman by the pot jabbered something. I looked hopeful. Fong shook his head. 'Ayee. No good.'

I said, 'What? What?'

The woman had lifted the lid now and was nodding and smiling at me. I nodded and smiled back.

Fong exploded frighteningly in Chinese at the woman, who cowered in her corner, then turned on me. 'No good for Missee and Boss.'

'Why not?' clutching at any straw, 'what is it?'

'Sour Fish Soup. No good. Only for tenants.' The shufflers looked carefully at the ground.

Soup is soup, I thought. Fish soup followed by lobster sounds like a theme.

'Come on Fong,' I wheedled. I looked over at the female.

She was nodding again, saying, 'OK, OK.'

Fong said, 'Ayee. Talkee talkee talkee.' The woman was already dishing soup into a tall jug. I grabbed it gratefully and headed for the door.

I heard Fong say something about 'lose *job*!' and called back, 'It's OK. I no tell Missee you.'

I made it back to the kitchen without incident and dumped the soup. Denver was gone and so was another half lobster, all the wine and several fingers of Remy. I raced to the music room and started lighting candles. I was about halfway, stuck on a difficult one, when the doorbell rang. I tried to keep going but it rang again, this time with a strong sense of urgency. A familiar voice from above screamed down, 'Paul! What the *hell's* going on down there? Someone's at the *door!*'

I abandoned the candles and hurried into the hall. I was still wearing my apron, but what the hell. I called up, 'It's OK!' with a reassuring calmness I was far from feeling.

I pushed back my hair and straightened my tie and took a deep breath, standing before the door for that moment which every performer needs before the curtain rises. The damn doorbell rang again and I tugged hard at all the handles.

The slab of California evening revealed by the door, which opened rather suddenly, was blotted out almost completely by a huge form. In full evening dress, complete with cloak, it might easily have been Count Dracula's giant brother. Beetle brows and a black widow's peak supported this alarming possibility. If this was Domingo Bananas, as indeed it turned out to be, he might well have earned his nombre from the great bunches of fingers he raised dramatically at our startling confrontation.

I bowed, not to be outdone in Gothic. 'Good eeevening, Sir.'

But it was when I raised my head that I received the greatest shock of the evening so far. Emerging from behind the dark cloud of Domingo was something shimmering in silver, all pale naked limbs and streaming hair.

'Hey, Paul. Well, whaddya know.' I couldn't speak. It was Suzanne.

— 6 —

'Honey, what the *hell* is this?'

We'd got through the music room scene, just about, but the champagne was warm and I was still wearing my apron. I knew the unlit candles hadn't gone unnoticed, either.

'Couldn't you have *dressed*? Was it *so* much trouble, you need to mortify me and my husband in front of our guests?' She was addressing me but looking at Suzanne.

'Ah think he looks just fahn!' Suzanne declared robustly, directing an absurdly dazzling smile at me. She held out her champagne flute and licked her lips. Her dress was a simple tier arrangement of short silver fringes which started on the lower slopes of her bosom and stopped soon afterwards on the upper slopes of her thighs.

Emboldened I flourished my bottle of non-quite-sufficiently-chilled Taittinger Blanc de Blanc and said, 'I thought my apron might lend a certain panache to my culinary efforts *ce soir.*'

'Y'all doin' the cookin'?' Suzanne's air of general incredulity and her accent were racing each other headlong for the limit.

'I sure am,' I assured her, stoutly confident.

'All on your ownsome?'

Out of the corner of my eye I could tell Jayne Belle was getting restless. All this fraternity between the help and a female guest, particularly one whose lack of clothes was making her feel uncomfortably overdressed, stuffed as she was into something brand new and tight, black and bright red from neck to knee, festooned with ropes of outsize pearls.

'Honey, did you put *any* vodka in this drink?' Jayne Belle didn't like champagne, chilled or not. She didn't like wine with meals either, preferring to stick to vodkas of steadily increasing strength, mixed in appropriate proportions with low-cal cranberry juice.

Suzanne chipped in at her, quite sharply, 'Don't y'all have a cook in a great place like this? Why, back home . . .'

We were mercifully distracted from this exchange by a sudden and violent fluctuation in light from the chandelier.

Kenny had abandoned the impassive Domingo after his small repertoire of conversational gambits had run out of steam, and was now stationed at the dimmer-switch, a favourite position, twiddling freely. The stuffed ambience of Louis quinze was thrown frightfully in and out of relief, like a sudden electrical storm in Mme de Montespan's boudoir. It maddened an already mad Jayne Belle.

'Do you *have* to do that?'

'It just don't seem right, somehow.' Kenny wore the velvet jacket. He wore it most evenings nowadays. There was a perplexed glint to his glasses.

'It was fine till you started screwin' around with it.'

I coughed gently. 'I think it might possibly be because not all the candles are lit, Sir.'

Kenny seemed to accept this, looking disconcerted rather than annoyed. He made a few final adjustments before resuming his seat and his attempts to charm Domingo. Charm was never Kenny's strong point.

Obviously Señor Domingo had something Kenny wanted, but it certainly wasn't small-talk. He had even less of it than Kenny, and that he was keeping to himself. Arrayed on the spindly French furniture he appeared more massive than ever, particularly next to a host one-fifth his size. Without the cloak he was no less Transylvanian, right down to the jewel-encrusted order at his throat. But his feet were oddly tiny, compared to the outsize banana hands, encased in leather pumps with silver buckles.

His manner was disconcerting, even to Kenny, and particularly to Jayne Belle, who liked a positive reaction from guests, especially male guests, to her home, the quality of her hospitality, her possessions, and her appearance. All anybody could get from Domingo Bananas was an occasional raising and lowering of the hands. Perhaps he didn't speak English.

Suddenly Kenny reached the end of his short fuse. 'Are we *ever* gonna eat?'

'It only remains for me to prepare the sauce, Sir,' I said, still fairly emboldened.

'Then whaddya hangin' around for?'

'It's all right, honey,' Jayne Belle was sweetly consoling, 'we'll take care of ourselves.' She pawed the air in my direction with jewelled languor.

'Right-oh, then.' Slightly crestfallen, but brave in the face of Suzanne, I bowed and prepared to leave.

'And honey?' Jayne Belle hit me with both barrels of her widest smile.

'Yes?'

'Get on with it.'

I got on with it but when I reached the door Suzanne was right there with me. 'I think the boy needs a little help from his friends.'

Jayne Belle and Kenny were too startled to speak. There was no perceptible change in Domingo.

Suzanne continued, 'Paul here's ma cookin' pardner, see.'

Jayne Belle gave me a look, both wounded and deeply accusatory, that stirred up guilt feelings I didn't even know I had. 'You never said . . .'

'Well, the poor guy,' (close up, Suzanne smelt of wild violets and honey) 'he's just a *butler*. He's not supposed to talk.'

'No, absolutely.' The old boldness was trickling back.

'Besides, the practice'll do me good. Señor Domingo wants me to be good, don't you, darlin'?'

Domingo raised his monolithic head and spread the hands. 'She sure need to do *something*,' he rumbled.

'Oh, I c'n do *something*, all right.' Suzanne unleashed a peal of silvery laughter that shook the chandelier and tightened Jayne Belle's smile to the absolute limit. 'C'mon, hun.' She grabbed my arm and we were gone.

Denver was back in the kitchen. We caught him in the act of sampling the soup. His whole face was wrung up like washing. 'What the . . .' Then he caught sight of Suzanne, 'Oh, my God!'

'This is Denver,' I said, helpfully.

'Hi, darlin',' Suzanne went right up to him. 'I'm Suzanne. I'm the new help.'

Denver gaped at me, hoping against hope. 'No way.'

I nodded and smiled.

'There is no *way* this girl is really going to work here . . .?'

'I'm workin' here tonight, hun. That's all that matters. What do *you* do?' Denver opened his mouth and grinned.

'Denver just *is*,' I said, 'Denver is an *is* person.'

Denver said, 'That's right. That's *right*!'

'Come on,' I said, 'we'd better get cracking. I'll heat up the soup.'

'No way,' said Denver, 'there is no way you're going to serve up that stuff to my mom.'

'Why not?'

'You will be *fired*, man. You will be *killed*.'

I sniffed it. 'Is it really that bad?'

'Oh, man, it is *revolting*. That soup is prob'bly the most disgusting and revolting thing in the history of the universe.'

Suzanne stuck her little finger into the soup, then wrinkled her nose. 'Yuk. I know! Let's put sumpn' in it.'

Denver said, 'Something heavy heavy duty.'

Suzanne said, 'How about whiskey?'

Denver said, 'Oh, *wow*. I can't believe this. This is the best. The *best*!'

'Call it "Southern Style".' Suzanne stood with her legs apart and looked boldly at me, with arched brows.

I said, 'Now, look . . .'

'Got any rye?' Suzanne chewed out the words at Denver in a tough way.

'How about Jack?'

'Groovy, baby.'

Denver disappeared at a run. Left alone in the kitchen with Suzanne I realised we had never been alone before. The feeling of intimacy seemed to evaporate. I felt stuffy and inhibited.

'You're going to get me in trouble, Suzanne.' I grinned awkwardly.

She made a sour face and flipped her fingers dismissively. 'I doubt it.'

I felt oddly and horribly depressed at this, but then Denver came bouncing back in with the bottle of Jack Daniels and the moment passed.

They poured in several healthy slugs, in between swigs. I left them to it and got the Lalique bowls ready to receive. Eventually they pronounced the mixture groovy but I didn't want to taste it.

'A tad of sour cream on top,' said Suzanne.

'Right on,' said Denver.

'Sprig of parsley?'

'Why not!'

The bell jangled furiously from the dining room. It was showtime. I felt my knees weaken. Suzanne seemed to read my mind. She came over to me, motherly and a little patronising. 'Don't worry, hun. Denver 'n I'll take in the soup. You leave it to us ole boys 'n get on with your sauce.'

Denver said, 'Oh, yeah. This is the *best*. This is prob'ly the best evening of my whole *life*. This is prob'ly the best girl in the whole history of the *world*. Paul, you are the greatest Red Butler of *all time*. Where did you *find* this girl?'

I tried to be jolly but I felt glum. I said, 'Denver, get *outa here*.'

They didn't come back.

Rather to my surprise my *sauce Americaine* seemed to turn out OK. As a concession to my operating solo, Jayne Belle had approved plate service.

I sliced lobster onto four plates and daubed it liberally with sauce. I added baby zucchinis, complete with flowers, which I hoped were al dente. I grabbed up two of the plates, took a deep breath and headed for the dining room.

Even before I shoved precariously through the sprung swing door I could tell the atmosphere had changed dramatically. Great shrieks and shouts of laughter filled the air.

The party was all bunched up at one end of the long refectory table, around their charming hostess (they must have moved their own placements). Suzanne was squeezed in between Denver and Domingo. Kenny was up and pouring, one hand on Domingo's shoulder, his glasses blazing with mirth. Domingo's face was raised to his, red lips splitting the bluish jowls, one hand on Suzanne.

'Denver has decided to join us, honey. Will you set a place for him, please?'

I was halfway through an aloof performance of the tricky 'pick-up-and-set-down' procedure at Suzanne's place, she being the female guest. I had a good view of where Domingo's hand was. She seemed impervious to both it and me, happily lapping up some mindless nonsense of Denver's.

My aloofness intensified as I picked up and set down before Jayne Belle. She could feel the vibe, I could tell, because she looked up sweetly and said, 'That soup was just *fabulous*.'

'Yeah,' Suzanne looked absently down the table at me, 'real creative.'

I bowed coldly and moved with as much dignity as possible to the sideboard, where it became necessary for me to kneel before its gothic extravagances and scrabble through its lower drawers for cutlery for Denver. I thought of the two (only) plates of lobster getting cold in the kitchen.

As I laid the equipment before Denver, Jayne Belle said,

sweeter than ever, 'Oh, and honey, get me another drink, would you?'

'Certainly.' The word slipped out like an icicle. Jayne Belle was really enjoying herself.

I headed for the door. I was about two-thirds through it when her voice stopped me again. 'Oh, honey . . .'

Stiffly I turned, very much the humble and obedient servant, eyebrows quivering question marks.

'Put on Denver's tape, would you, please? We'd all *so* much like to hear it.'

Everyone got looser to the beat of the Hot Hebrews. Domingo fairly exuded beneficence, to Kenny's obvious joy, like a vampire gorged on blood. Whether or not he really liked the Hot Hebrews was hard to say. Unlike Suzanne and Denver, he wasn't dancing. A couple more vodkas and Jayne Belle was dancing with them. Kenny and Domingo went into a huddle.

I managed to get loose too, by myself in my pantry, on sweet and stupifying Poire Williams, which reminded me of the gripe water Nanny used to prescribe for every ill. Unfortunately, looseness of mind and body were not an advantage when Kenny announced his intention of calling up the spirit of Napoleon.

This was a ritual which demanded my services in a testing performance role. I wasn't sure if I was up to it.

I wasn't the only one alarmed by the proposal. My ally at least was in a stronger position to voice her objections.

'Honey, our guests don't want to sit through that crap!'

'How do you know?' Kenny got belligerent.

'Because they're not brain-dead, you jerk.'

'Ya wanna see my statue of Napoleon?' Kenny turned to Domingo for support.

Domingo flapped a banana or two. 'With the greatest of pleasure, *mi amigo*.'

Pride of place in the forest of classical statuary crowding Kenny's private circus maximus went to the Emperor Napoleon Bonaparte, 'Enthroned in Glory'.

Special foundations had been sunk deep in the priceless Beverly Hills ground beneath Kenny's office to support the great man. He sat, twice-lifesize, in folds of marble like soft Italian ice-cream, white as snow and death, imperial oak leaves at his brow, his robe embroidered with Charlemagne's bees, orb and sceptre held firmly in his hands. His chin was sunk on his chest. 'So grim,' Kenny pronounced, as he often did, looking up at the liberating tyrant with quiet awe. It was a grimness he strove to emulate, with some success, to keep at bay those who would part him from his money, or seek to prevent him from amassing more. 'A great man.'

'A very great man!' Domingo seemed enthusiastically in tune with Kenny now, his stiff front melted. Perhaps he was just shy. He appeared more human still in the presence of the man who had once said, '*L'Europe, c'est moi.*' He said, 'That guy sure knew how to get things moving.'

Kenny said, 'He sure did. Paul here knows plenty about Napoleon.'

'Oh, I wouldn't say that.' I was still hoping for a reprieve.

That faint hope became fainter when Suzanne drawled, 'C'mon, Paul, lay some culture on us.'

'Yeah, man,' Denver's slurred contribution was equally unwelcome, 'shock it to ush.'

'Hold it, hold it,' Kenny took charge. 'The lighting! Paul, get the lights!'

The Victor of Lodi and Marengo would have extracted grim satisfaction from knowing that, despite stiff competition from the likes of Caesar Augustus and Pompey the Great, he alone in Kenny Graumann's Hall of Fame had his own lighting system.

On the master panel behind the Emperor, I cut the main lights in the room. The golden blaze faded to black as Jayne Belle's voice rose in shrill dismay. 'Paul, I *forbid* you to do this!'

'Go ahead, Paul.' Kenny's voice was imperious in the darkness.

'Impossible is only a word!' I cried, getting in the mood. I twiddled the Imperial rheostat, creating a ghostly glow.

'Great! Great! Go on, Paul, say some more stuff.' Kenny, although strictly speaking a money- rather than a film-maker, liked to put on a good show. Inside most producers is a director wanting to get out.

'What sort of stuff, Sir?' My brain was throbbing horribly and I was stalling.

'You know what sort of stuff, goddammit! Tell us the one about how he came back from that island.'

'You mean, "Who will be the first man to shoot his Emperor", Sir?'

'That's it! That's it. Tell us about that.'

Jayne Belle, seething in the dark, said, 'Not that. We heard that enough times already.'

'They didn't hear it, did they? Company didn't hear it. Go ahead, Paul.'

We went through the Nice landing, backtracked to the scenes of grief with the Old Guard at the abdication, the journey from Moscow in the Red Sledge, ending up with how the Emperor had struck the word 'impossible' from the French dictionary.

'Summa these union guys could use that idea,' Kenny wise-cracked. I saw him lean across to Domingo in the dimness, 'Don't worry, Domingo. We'll make this picture non-union. Leave it to me.'

'I gotta faith in you, baby. Just like the Old Guard.'

This inspired Kenny. 'Go on, Paul!' He was feeling feverishly close to the source now, I could tell. Through half-closed eyes in the eerie light he could see his Emperor glimmering, coming alive. He could hear the fabric flutter as the Imperial standards unfurled, thunder of Jerome's cavalry, thunder of Soult's guns.

Hidden behind the marble I threw forth a voice I hoped approximated to Bonaparte's: harsh, hoarse, rallying, shot through with passion. My own hackles prickled as I unleashed the lines I knew Kenny most wanted to hear.

'Impossible is only a word! To the coward it is a refuge, to the timid a ghost, but, believe me, in the mouth of power, it is merely a declaration of impotence!'

When, finally, clinging to the open front door for support, I let our visitors out, the bonhomie was undiminished. As they picked their way, heads twisting back, faces split with last smiles and final cries, Suzanne's compact ass was snugly obscured by one vast banana hand. I was so tired I didn't care.

What Jayne Belle remembered about the evening, my part of it anyway, was apparently good, because she told me my cooking classes were to continue. The dinner had been good. Fabulous, in fact. Especially the soup.

Next week found me back at Rojay's bungalow on south La Brea. From several blocks away I could see the white Rolls, taking up most of Rojay's parking, top down despite cool winter weather. I parked, hitting the kerb, preoccupied with how it would be seeing Suzanne, how she would be, how I should be. I walked in and stood in the inner doorway, my eyes recovering from the outside brightness, involuntarily hunting the room.

I felt a tight little thud in my upper chest when I saw her. I had to look twice. Her honey hair was pulled back tight, tied in a bun. She wore a navy Chanel pantsuit, complete with creamy blouse, gold bracelets and necklace, flat, matching leather shoes with gold buckles. I wasn't sure if I could see her shining through it all or not, ready or not to bust out. If you ignored the glow she was a perfect match for the matron with whom she had today been paired, or had paired herself, I didn't know. I was drinking it all in, I suppose, in a cloud, when the reverie was rudely interrupted by Rojay. He got right up to me before I spotted him.

'Don't even dream about it, sweetnutsssss!' he hissed, straight into my ear.

'Huh?'

'You know fickin' well what I'm saying. Fickin' little Miss Scarlett O'Whore-a over there.'

'Look . . .' I finally got up to date with his act, '*fuck off,* Rojay!' We were both hissing now, at each other's throats at last, only in undertones.

'Oh . . . Oh, baby, so you wanna play rough, hey?'

'I don't want to play at all, actually.'

'Well let me just tell *you*, you big fickin' old British *whore* . . . big whore in silly trousers, let me tell you . . .' He was beside himself.

I was all drawn up to my full height. 'Tell me what?'

'You think you're so fickin' superior! You're trash. *Trash*! Like everybody else in this town. Trash like me. You're no better than me, you know that?'

'I never said I was.'

'I can get you fired any time. Right? Just say the word.'

Suddenly I felt awfully tired. 'Look, Rojay . . .'

'Just say one word to that cheap trashy little piece a pussy over there an' I tell Jayne Belle and . . . Pouff!' Rojay made an exploding gesture with his arms. It couldn't easily go unnoticed and it didn't. I looked uneasily around. Panstick faces split by brilliant orthodonty were raised, bright and questioning, towards us.

'It's OK, girls!' Rojay was instantly his old playful self.

'Just a minor culinary contretemps!' I boomed. Rojay's arm snaked around my shoulder. He was right. We were two of a kind, no better than each other.

On my way to my solitary corner I passed within brushing distance of Suzanne. Her absorption seemed both light-hearted and absolute. No warning from Rojay was needed to stop my mouth. I looked at her first boldly, then shiftily, and passed on.

She entered with wholehearted enthusiasm into the lesson *du jour* (*noisettes d'agneau aux truffes* followed by pecan pie). She had a lot to say about pecans. I hung dully in my booth, never catching her eye. After a while, I didn't look at anybody, just got on with it. That's what I was there for. I thought, 'Scarlett O'Whore-a. Hmmm. Not bad, that.'

I got home at five. There was a message stuck baldly to my apartment door: RING YOUR WIFE.

Tension clamped my neck and temples, a small headache sprang into action, my mouth went dry, my ears sang. Fong said something but his voice seemed far away.

I disappeared into my room, sat on the bed end and stared at the phone. What could it be? I looked at my watch. She must have got up early to call me, long before the hours of economy.

A low-voltage tremor ran through my fingers as they moved haltingly around the digits. My tension mounted through the usual international noises, increasing at the first ring. It was ringing, at least. I would soon know. I hunkered down for the interminable wait. To distract myself I started half-consciously to empty my pockets. I would need to change from my day uniform into my evening one. I pulled out the usual change and keys and screwed up till rolls and old, yellow messages. The phone was still ringing as I checked the side pockets of my jacket. I didn't keep anything there, to avoid unsightly bulges which upset Jayne Belle. I pulled out a square of stiff paper and stared at it absently. It was the torn top half of a tab from Le Dôme. Puzzled, but still only half aware, I turned it over. Something was scribbled in red biro on the back. As I started to decipher it I woke up abruptly to what it was. At that moment the ringing stopped and a breathless voice said, 'Hallo!' It was Natasha.

I couldn't answer. I was still staring at the piece of paper.

'Hallo? Hallo? Paul, is that you?'

'Hallo? Natasha?'

'Thank God. Why didn't you answer?'

'How are you, Natasha?'

'I'm OK. How are you?'

'Fine.' I was still staring hypnotically, somewhere between horror and extreme joy, at a telephone number and an address in Venice, CA. She wrote her sevens, I noticed, the continental way. 'Is anything wrong?'

'Only the usual.'

'How d'you mean, "the usual"?'

'I mean there isn't any *money*, Paul.'

'But Natasha, I send you money all the time.'

'Yes, but it isn't *enough*. You don't know what it's *like*. Mummy keeps on at me, and the schools. Oh, God, Paul,' her voice was breaking down, 'I can't stand it . . . we've got nothing. Nothing . . .' The last word was a great, dry, sob.

'Look, Natasha, I'm sure soon . . .' I felt remorse, anger, pity, regret, but hardly any of the hope I wished to transmit.

'Paul, I've got something serious to say.' She had pulled herself together, sounded brisk, strange, a stranger. 'You may not like it . . .'

I felt blood drain from my face, still staring at Suzanne's note, but it had lost its lustre, offered no comfort. 'It's about that fucker Nigel, isn't it!'

There was a long silence. The line hummed. My angry words echoed back at me with inhuman cosmic mockery. I thought I could hear her muffled whispers.

'Natasha? Are you there? Who are you talking to?'

'It's only Mummy. It's all *right*, Mummy. I'm going to tell him *now*.'

'Tell me *what*?'

'It's just that Mummy thinks . . . well, Nigel's offered me this job – '

'I knew it! What sort of job?'

'A sort of personal assistant, you know. A PA . . .' She finished lamely.

'I don't know what possible sort of job you could do for that bastard, except a blow job. And you're not much good at that.'

'Paul!'

'That's it, isn't it? You're *fucking* the guy.'

'He's offering to pay me a really good salary.'

'I *bet* he is!'

'It'll make all the difference, Paul, honestly.'

'Why ask me about it? I don't know why you bother.'

'It's just that it means I'll have to go away with him quite a lot. You know, when he goes off on trips.'

I could hear someone screaming in my tiny room, 'Natasha you *bitch*, you fucking *whore*! Do what you fucking *like*!' I threw the receiver at the instrument, shocked as I did so at my own violence. I was shaking all over. I sat and watched it for a while, waiting for it to ring back. It didn't. Then I went into the bathroom and threw up.

Later on I padded around the dining room table, as was both necessary and usual. The role slipped on easily, like a woolly vest. I was a wounded wolf in warm sheep's clothing.

'A little more wine, Sir?'

'Thanks.'

It was just Jayne Belle and Kenny tonight, a homely dinner for two of game hen with a foie gras stuffing.

'This is *fabulous*, honey.'

'I got the idea from Rojay.'

'He's a *genius*. Don't you think so, Kenny?'

Kenny said, 'Did you get these game hens from Phil's?'

'Yes, Sir.'

'What did you pay for them?'

'Er . . .'

'Can you lay *off*? You wanna nickle and dime everyone to *death*, that's your trouble. No wonder nobody *likes* you.' Jayne Belle gave me a bright, protective smile. I smiled back. She said, 'What did your wife want?'

'Oh . . . nothing.'

The look was still bright, but the smile was gone. 'You know, honey, what you need most in your life is a *job*.'

Kenny looked up, his glasses alight. He was attracted by the possibilities of this line of reasoning. 'That's *right*. Who needs a wife? Who can *afford* one?'

Jayne Belle looked down the table at him with withering contempt. Kenny didn't notice. He was back attacking the game hen, sucking every bone clean of precious meat.

'Honey,' Jayne Belle infused the look with plenty of warmth. I gangled before her, a slack, receptive smile on my face. 'You know there'll *always* be a home for you here.'

Winter in Los Angeles. The rains can come in January and February, to the unfailing bewilderment of southern Californians, washing astronomical real estate down impossible slopes, reducing the arterial brain of freeways to a soaking twilight zone of carnage.

But November is often sweet Indian spring. It was like that the day I first drove to Venice to see Suzanne. Cool air trickled like wine over the tongue, mellow sun warm across the shoulders. Kenny and Jayne Belle went out to lunch at the Bistro Garden and I got the rest of the day off. It's such a nice day, honey, you deserve it.

I was still in uniform. I'd forgotten what being out of it was like. Natives in bright Bermudas and brown torsos were like alien beings to me. I despised and envied them at the same time, hiding behind my obsequious, authoritative facade. I felt safe, like a Norman in his castle, peeping out through arrow slits at a potentially hostile and unpredictable world. I liked my uniform. I didn't like taking it off. I'd become institutionalised.

I cruised down the Santa Monica freeway and got onto Ocean, going south. On the phone Suzanne had said hang a right on Rose, which you get to when things begin looking funky.

If Los Angeles has a Chelsea, it is Venice. Venice feels Victorian, has canals, is on the beach. The megalomaniac dream of some bygone mogul to recreate the City of the Doges on God's own Little Acre, it has sunk and silted its way into being an all-year-round carnival, a shoddy and hilarious parody of itself — an American dream that went wrong and became for once a joke and not a nightmare. Venice is overrun with strip pine and patchouli-scented boutiques run by laid back people in wide-brim leather hats reminiscent of Haight Ashbury in its heyday. The wooden walkways rumble to the wheels of nearly nude rollerskaters. Nearly nude gays pump iron in enclosures on the beach.

It has an authentic junkie drop-out element, which presumably will be cleared out soon in the name of soaring real estate values. Meanwhile the place is still truly groovy, the natural habitat of hipsters, with a liberal sprinkling of avant garde art galleries, condo-loads of young, upwardly mobile actors and attorneys, and no shortage of classy restaurants with fancy New York prices for them to hang out in.

I hung my right on Rose. Hang another at the bottom, she said, before the boardwalk. There's a little beach road. Don't mind the No Entries. Well, I was too stiff minded for that. I parked and walked. It was a track, really, back fences overhung with banana, vine and fig. It was a quiet, secret place, cut off immediately you set foot in it from the hubbub of mainstream Venice. Ambling along, I breathed it all in, undid my jacket and peered for numbers. There didn't seem to be any. A wooden garage door was tilted halfway up. The back of the white Rolls told me I had reached journey's end.

At last I felt nervous. My mouth went dry. Alone with Suzanne, properly alone for the first time, without props — what was I doing? We were complete strangers, really. Aliens. I felt alien at the back gate, fumbling at the latch. It was wooden, with a leather thong. No locks, buzzers, bells, intercoms, the usual paraphernalia of LA life. As it swung open I became more deeply conscious of the formality of my attire. With a wild movement I tugged off my tie and bunched it into my pocket. I was in a little, wild garden, paved with old mosaic tiles, bright blue, cream and red. A fountain plashed on red terracotta in the centre, water glittering like hot jewels. Sun came pouring through the trellis above, hung with grapes, overhung with bougainvillaea.

Flowers and ferns burst everywhere out of pots, suckled by bees, fluttered over by bright, gaudy butterflies. Breathing in what was so hot and damp and fertile, it was like being at the potent beginning of things. I felt very conscious of being far from naked, in that garden.

Suzanne came out of the back of the house through some open french windows. I could hear Tom Petty playing behind her, 'Strangered in the Night'. She held a glass of white wine in one hand. It flashed with sunbeams. She put her bare toes gingerly on the hot tiles, saying, 'Hi! Welcome to the unreal world.'

I said, 'Hi, Suzanne,' and put my hands in my pockets. She wore a hot pink tank top and loud, geometric patterned bermuda shorts with laces at the fly. Her midriff and her legs were bare.

We walked towards each other and I kissed her. I started to peck her cheek but she pushed her face awkwardly against mine. Her hair was pale and wispy, blown all over her face, smelling of shampoo. I found her mouth through wet strands of hair. Her lips opened warmly. The surface of her tongue was rough and tasted of wine.

I felt my body shake as my arms went around her. There was nothing I could do. I held on tight, digging my fingers into the backs of her shoulders, pulling back her head by her hair. She was still hanging on to the glass of wine.

My hands slid down her flanks and started tugging at her shorts. She said, 'Hold on,' and started backing slowly into the house. When I stopped tugging she said, 'Mmmmm, mmmm, it's OK. Keep goin'. I just don't wanna be so public, is all.'

Inside the room was light and cool with a white wood floor and shut venetian blinds the other end. There was no furniture, except a sun lounger, a stereo, some books lying around, an open bottle of wine on the stone hearth of a fireplace full of dried flowers.

Suzanne tilted down and put her wine glass carefully on the floor. As she came up she placed her hands over mine at her waist. Gyrating slightly she tugged gently at the shorts, expertly loosening the strings as she did so. She raised one knee and the shorts were gone. I felt my hands on cool flesh, like silky marble.

She moved backwards towards the sun lounger, kicking the shorts away, leading me loosely by the hands. She sat down, looking up at me. I stood there looking down, not moving, not even daring to think. She crossed her hands over her chest, like a bishop, and pulled the tank top over her head. Then she moved back along the seat, resting her back, hanging her hair over the end and shaking it out of her face. She kept her eyes mesmerically on mine. She was smiling. Her knees were up, and, as I watched, they slowly parted. She looked down. I looked down. We looked at that part of her which was also hot and damp and fertile.

I felt overdressed again. She looked back up at me. She seemed very young, a little confused, a little embarrassed by what she'd done. Her voice when it came was strange, like someone else's voice. It had lost all its boldness, was smaller and slightly unsure.

'I think this is what you need, isn't it, Paul?'

I nodded slowly. I couldn't speak.

She laughed. I could hear the relief, 'Well come *on*, darlin'. Ain't I done enough? I don't know how to seduce you any further. No man *ever* had so much encouragement as this. What does it take to get you out of that darned ole uniform? Go on! Take it off! I think it's demeanin'!'

I struggled and tugged and hopped my way out of my clothes. It was hard to know which looked sillier, the uniform or me. Certainly, seeing it there in a heap on the floor, Suzanne's seemed a good word for it. Those striped trousers were hardly peacock feathers.

Suzanne retrieved her wine and enjoyed the show, 'Look at you! You're all big'n flabby under there!'

I sat down sheepishly on the edge of the sun lounger. She snorted with laughter. I said, 'What's the matter?' trying to sound nonchalant and not too irritated.

'Looks like a Catch-22 situation.'

'How d'you mean?'

'This thing ain't gonna hold the both of us. You're a big boy.'

I smiled down at her, putting my hand on one squashy breast. I wanted to be dominant and masculine, but being naked was beginning to feel like being nudists now, after all the excitement. I kissed her and said, 'Well?'

'I guess we could re-pair to the bedroom. If you insist.'

We trooped through in single file, two slightly shorter people with big bottoms and flat feet. Her bedroom was like a clothing store that has recently been ransacked. All the cupboard doors were open wide. An ornate mirrored vanity table against one wall was crowded with a thousand bottles and jars. We picked our way across to a kingsize four-poster with a frilly top. Suzanne went ahead and jumped on the bed, striking an abandoned posture. I jumped on after her, pinning her down dramatically.

There were only sheets on the bed, and giant pillows. Sheets and pillowcases were all made of apricot satin. It seemed sensuous, but in practice was extremely slithery. I grappled with Suzanne and she with me. We were both enthusiastically willing, but it didn't seem possible to get a real purchase on anything for long. We slithered around for a while and then stopped, out of breath.

Suzanne blinked up at me, 'I guess you're just out of practice.'

I groaned. 'It's this bed. It's much too slippery.'

She stretched and yawned. 'I just don't turn you on, I guess.'

This had me up, with some difficulty, into a crouch. I looked down at her with burning sincerity. 'Of *course* you do, Suzanne. You turn me on like *mad*.'

'Coulda fooled me.'

I twisted onto my back. 'I know what you mean. It is pretty surprising, I admit.' I looked at her sideways. 'I'd've thought being in bed with you would be about the most exciting thing in the world.'

'And it isn't?'

'No, it is. Of course it is. It's just . . . I just don't seem to be able to take it seriously, that's all.'

'Thanks a *bunch*!'

'No, I mean . . . I don't know what I mean. Suzanne, listen.' I got up on one elbow. 'I just feel so at home with you, that's part of the trouble. So familiar. Can you understand that?'

'Oh, I'm too dumb to, I expect. Just a dumb broad.'

I hoisted myself up more, looking down into her face. She was flushed pink under her tan, her eyes bright, smiling. 'If I said . . .' Her chin went down and her eyebrows went up very slightly. I continued, 'If I said . . . I liked you too much . . . would that sound . . . absolutely awful?'

It was quite a relief when she laughed. 'My God!' She watched me for a while, then put out a hand to my cheek. It felt cool. She said, 'You know what I think? I think you like your *wife* too much. That's the trouble with *you*.'

So in the end I lay on that sexy bed in that exquisite beach house beside all that ravishing beauty and told her about Nigel. Through the window the merry throng rolled by along the boardwalk, laughing to the sound of their ghettoblasters.

Suzanne listened intently to my sorry tale. At the finish she said, 'Well, I think she's a real lucky gal.'

'Ha! I'm sure *she* thinks so!'

'She will, you wait. Right now she doesn't know what to do. You love her. Have a little faith.'

'You don't know that slimebag Nigel.'

'She chose *you*. Never forget that. A girl can't ever change her mind about a thing like that.'

'I think she's sleeping with him.'

'You're sleepin' with me!'

'Not very successfully!'

'I don't expect she'll do it very successfully with Nigel.'

'You think she'll do it, then?'

'Hell, I don't know, Paul. C'mon. This is gittin' borin'.'

'Sorry.'

'I know!' Suzanne brightened and jumped off the bed. 'Speakin' of infidelity, let's do some of Domingo's drugs.'

Suzanne unscrewed the top of a gold makeup pencil and poured shiny crystals onto the glass top of the vanity table. 'Bet you ain't never seen rocks like these.'

I shook my head.

'Only the *real* megastars get this stuff.'

'Is Domingo a real megastar?'

'Come *on*, hun. You mean you ain't twigged about Domingo yet?'

I glanced around, shrugging off my innocence. 'He pays for all this, I suppose?'

'A girl has to live. It sure beats Seventh Avenue.'

I sat on the edge of the bed, looking wise, trying to imagine what happened on Seventh Avenue.

'We're a couple of birds in gilded cages,' I said, finally.

'Domingo's a bird in a private jet, a high flyin' bird. What the hell d'you think he's launderin' with that ole boss o' yours?' Suzanne was busy at the vanity table with her gold card.

'He's putting money into some movie of his, I thought.'

'That's right.' Suzanne looked at me oddly. 'You goddit. Come on, Paul, if we're gonna get paranoid, let's get paranoid.'

Later on, the cool garden deep in blue shadow, the fountain pattering in the stillness, chopper blades suddenly churned the air overhead. Suzanne ran indoors and dived under the bed. 'It's him! I *know* it's him!'

'Don't be crazy. It's just the sheriffs, or something.'

'Oh, Paul, you don't know what you're doing to me. You just don't know. Your car's not outside, is it?' Her face was hollow with fear.

'No. I parked on Rose.'

'Thank God.'

The chopper went away, but Suzanne wouldn't come out

from under the bed for some time. She said, 'D'you have to be back tonight?'

'I guess not.'

'Would you stay here? I feel kinda weird.'

Much later, warm together under the satin, she said, 'What you need is to pour a little money on the wound.'

I knew just what she meant. Cosy as I was I could still hear Natasha's desperate voice. 'But *what* money?'

'Whatever you're gittin' in that loonytune joint, you're underpaid. You really know how to handle it. You're a *natural*. They'd never find another freak like you in a million years. You just gotta *go for it*.'

In the darkness Tom Petty and the Heartbreakers were playing quietly, 'Even the Losers'. The wise words of Doctor Love came back to me: a double boost. I stretched and turned in my slippery hollow. 'OK.'

'A *raise*? What are you, *crazy*?!!!' Jayne Belle's face was leathery and gaunt with outrage.

'Certainly not.' My attempt to be brisk and businesslike deteriorated into sullenness.

'How could you do this to me?'

'Look, come *on*.'

'It'll kill my husband!'

'I don't see why.'

'After all we've done for you. You haven't even been here a year.'

'I've been here almost a year. Things are desperate.'

'Salaries can only be reviewed annually. Ask my husband.'

'All right, I will.'

'Don't get cute with *me*, honey.'

'No, I mean, seriously, don't you think I should?'

'He'll almost certainly let you go.'

'Well . . .' Somehow I had to keep pushing. 'We'll just have to see.'

Late that evening the intercom in the apartment buzzed. I had just given up and gone to bed.

'My husband will see you now.'

Hurrying upstairs in my hastily assembled garments, my heart beat like a drum. I cursed their psychological advantage, and cursed again when, two steps from the top, I tripped on a shoelace.

The boudoir door stood open, framing Jayne Belle in face pack and towelling robe. 'Don't look at me! *Honey*!!' she bawled over her shoulder into Kenny's lair. 'It's *Paul*.'

'What does *he* want?!'

'He wants to *see* you.'

'It's *late* already.'

Jayne Belle gave me her helpless little girl shrug. 'You wouldn't see him before.'

Kenny's sigh was audible all the way through the wall. 'Well . . .' The weight of the world was in the word. 'I guess I'll have to see him now, then.'

Jayne Belle turned her tragic white clown mask on me once more. All the twelve tribes of Israel rebuked me from her dark, mournful eyes. 'You better go in.'

Kenny too wore a towelling robe, identical to Jayne Belle's but for the blue 'K' embroidered on the pocket in place of her pink 'JB'. He was perched astride his exercise bike, pedalling furiously. His glasses blazed on his bright red face as he perused a copy of *Business Week* propped on a music stand.

I closed the door behind me and stood there, temporarily unmanned. I cleared my throat. Kenny looked up but kept on pedalling. 'What's on ya mind, Paul?'

'Didn't, er . . . didn't Mrs Graumann tell you, Sir?'

He shook his head. Little beads of sweat flew off.

'Well, it's like this, Sir, you see . . .'

'Bottom line, Paul. Cut the crap and gimme the bottom line.'

'Well, Sir, I need a raise.'

'What's that you say?' He had stopped pedalling abruptly. Without the whirr of the heavy flywheel the room was suddenly appallingly silent.

'A raise, Sir. A substantial one.'

Kenny's hands flew to his chest. Terrified thoughts of his triple bypass leapt to my mind. His head snapped back. Blue stubble glistened under his chubby chin. His mouth opened like a cave and out came a sound which raised every hair on my body: an animal sound, and a primitive, primeval, pre-historic animal at that.

After delivering himself of the Shrie Kenny fell off the bike and lay on the floor. The door burst open and Jayne Belle came howling in. 'What the *hell*'ve you done to my husband?'

'But I only – '

'How *could* you?!' Her black eyes blazed at me. Kenny's arms and legs were twitching feebly.

'But I simply said I needed a raise.' My voice was hushed but still insistent.

'I *told* you it would kill him!' Jayne Belle hissed.

I shook my head.

'Quick!' Fetch a glass of water!'

Glad to have an order to obey I hurried to fetch one and poured it down Kenny's throat. We assisted the billionaire into an armchair. He was moaning softly. I retrieved his glasses and replaced them on his face.

Kenny sipped more of his water and began slowly shaking his head. He murmured something. Jayne Belle leaned close, 'What's that, honey?'

'The guilt.'

'What's he say?' She looked at me in confusion.

'He says it's the guilt, I think.'

'What do you mean, sweetheart?' Jayne Belle addressed him tenderly. Kenny took a bolder sip from his glass. 'I would feel too guilty if I paid Paul any more.'

'Ya hear that? Ya *hear* that?!' Jayne Belle blazed at me, pulling at the front of her robe, which was falling open. 'You . . . *murderer*!!'

But something inside me had become determined. 'I'm sorry, Sir. I don't quite follow you.'

Kenny fixed a lens on me in which a faint glint was discernible. He was beginning to look much more like his old self. 'People are starving out there,' he said, waving a limp, exquisitely manicured hand in the general direction of Beverly Hills. 'How can I live with myself employing a fifty-thousand-a-year domestic?'

'I was thinking more of seventy-five, Sir. I already get almost fifty.'

'*Fifty per cent*?! You're asking *fifty per cent*?!!'

'Otherwise I can't go on. I'm doing this to try and keep my family together. Right now, on my present pay, it isn't working.'

'Your family? *Your* family?' Jayne Belle's mask was cracking and white powder filled the air around her face. 'What about *my* family, goddammit? You've damn near *killed* my husband!'

At the words 'fifty per cent' Kenny had relapsed and resumed moaning. Now he lifted his head and announced, not without a trace of triumph. 'Anyways, I won't be needing Paul.'

'*What*!!' Jayne Belle and I yelped pretty well in unison.

'I have to go back east.'

'Back *east*!' All fears for her husband's health deserted Jayne Belle. She blazed away at him as only she knew how. 'What the *hell* d'you mean you're going back east?'

'I just heard from Sammy. The money's firmed up and we start shooting. First, we have to check some locations.'

'Where? For chrissakes *why*? *Nobody* makes pictures back east except Woody Allen!'

Kenny shrugged. 'It's that kinda picture. Anyways,' a crafty look creeping over his face, 'Pennsylvania's non-union.'

'Pennsylvania!'

Talking mainly to himself now, Kenny continued, 'Some scenes *have* to be shot in New York. I figure I might get some city bucks from Ed for those . . .'

'And what about *me*?!' Jayne Belle's robe really was falling open now as she leaned into Kenny's face. She didn't care.

He looked up in surprise from his calculating reverie.

'Won't *I* need Paul? I suppose I can just fend for myself

— 134 —

while you're gone? Send for takeouts? Wash up?!'

'Paul can stay on here at his present salary if he wants or he can go home to his precious family or whatever. I don't care. It's up to him.'

'*Right*!' I heard my own disembodied voice boom loudly in my ears. 'That's *it*! Fuck *you*! Fuck you *all*! I *quit*!!' And I stormed out, slamming the boudoir door behind me, and thundered down the stairs.

Sitting alone on my bed in my black room, mine no longer, I noticed I was trembling. My hands were cold and I felt sick. I tried to consider the awful reality of what I had done to myself, but it was beyond consideration. Shock alone was keeping me from total disintegration. An awful silence filled the huge house.

My door flew open and crashed against the wall. Jayne Belle stood framed in it, breathing hard. Some of her mask had peeled away, but the comic possibilities of this were overshadowed by her general air of menace. She had changed into her grey exercise sweats.

'You are *not quitting*!!'

'Er . . .'

'Do you *hear me*?!'

A large wooden coathanger, the sort with heavy shoulder-blades, the expensive sort, employed to minimise crumpling of my soupstained finery, lay at the foot of the bed. Jayne Belle grabbed it and proceeded to rain violent blows from it to any exposed parts of me she could land on. I defended myself as best I could. 'Isn't it enough I should be abandoned by my *husband*?! I am *not* (WHACK) *going* (WHACK) to be *abandoned* (WHACK) by *you* (WHACK)!'

I slid from the bed to the floor and lay there, my arms over my head.

'Do you *hear* me?!!' She threw the hanger onto my back. I lay on, shaking and sobbing either with pain or laughter or both, I wasn't sure. In muffled tones I managed a strangled question. 'What about my raise?'

— 135 —

'Another twenty grand and that's *it*.'
I closed my eyes in an ecstasy of relief.

During the morning of the first day of Kenny's absence Jayne Belle paraded the bliss of being what she called a 'single woman' at length and to anyone who would listen. In the case of the domestic staff listening was compulsory, and could be done at the same time as supplying her with the ever-increasing number of goods and services her solitude demanded. In the case of Denver, he quit the house early, rising well before noon, claiming a pressing need for rehearsals with the Hot Hebrews.

By early afternoon a succession of people started arriving to assist in the process of relaxation: Jayne Belle's manicurist, her pedicurist, her foot-reflexologist, her masseuse. At four her doctor arrived. A possible lump had been detected during her massage. He left soon after, having given the all-clear. Jayne Belle celebrated with an iced tea, a chicken sandwich and a tuna salad.

At five-thirty the work-out guy arrived, and she tore down to the gym. My trained eye told me that the relaxation process was by now going downhill at breakneck speed and promised to come off the rails at any moment. Taking the initiative I hit the panic button and called her mother:

'How would you like to come over to dinner tonight?'

'I would hate to. What's wrong?'

'I can arrange for there to be rack of lamb and *crême brulée.*'

'Cut the crap. What's up?'

'I think your daughter might be missing her husband.'

'She hates her husband. She called me and told me so.'

'She did?'

'She called me eighteen times today arready.'

'That's what I mean.'

'I don't see. I don't wanna see.'

— 136 —

'I mean, I think she's bored.'

'You think I don't know my own daughter? I *know* she's bored. I just don't want to be the one to unbore her. Is that a word?'

'You call her and invite yourself. I think she'd be pleased.'

'You think *you'd* be pleased, you mean. What am I, some kinda service industry?'

'You are her mother. She needs you.'

Not long after, the work-out over, I took the call myself and put Iris through. Jayne Belle screamed over the bannisters, '*Mother's Coming to Dinner. You Better Make it Good*!'

I arranged the promised lamb-rack and *crème brulée* with a recalcitrant and dark-complexioned Fong.

During the ensuing tête-a-tête, tended by me as with some rare desert flower, lubricated with exquisite nutrients, illuminated by flickering candles and odd, well-chosen passages of English wit, Jayne Belle had the first of her inspirational ideas: something she could really throw herself into.

'Paul, what the *hell* is happening with that goddam Sistine Chapel? I haven't seen any action for *months*!'

From now on we saw plenty.

The truth was that Kenny had never liked the scheme. By sitting in his office he had been able effectively to block it, since a portion of his back wall needed to be knocked down to accommodate the chapel. Now, with her husband gone, Jayne Belle was able to get at both it and him. This she did with all the pent up frenzy built up inside her since his announcement. Lethal in headband and sweats, she took personal charge of the manpower. The office must be cleared. *Cleared*. It was as if all trace of the miscreant were to be eradicated.

Like galley slaves we laboured, Hoobey, Werner, Fong and I, under Jayne Belle's fearsome eye and Boothby Cunningham's languid one. Slowly the great monument to human pride emptied itself of its mighty contents and the gym filled up, until all that remained was Napoleon, the rock, solitary as St Helena on his immovable foundation, a persistent reminder of the missing tyrant.

The great day dawned when the sledgehammers could be applied. By eleven o'clock that morning all was in readiness. Champagne, the most expensive the cellar could disgorge, was chilled in generous quantities. Massimo di Los Angeles, complete with cherubic acolytes, arrived in good time to help Jayne Belle, her mother, and Boothby Cunningham drink it.

Jayne Belle herself took the first swipe. An especially small, clean sledgehammer was provided. She swung it with all the might of an Olympic hammer-thrower on steroids. She kept on swinging, until plaster gave way to brick and the mounting dustcloud drove her finally, triumphantly back.

Hoobey's team of born-again misfits took over under the critical eye of Boothby. Fong and I were released to our duties, which that afternoon included the preparation of an authentic English tea. Fong had been trained in Hong Kong by British rulers and had unwisely boasted to Jayne Belle one day of his ability to make scones and other delicacies favoured by the Island Race. With my natural hereditary aptitude for the conceptual role and Fong's for the cooking one it seemed a match made in heaven.

Boothby and Iris had been invited to stay during this difficult time, so it was the least we could do, wasn't it, to keep them amused and entertained with a relentless succession of treats.

We laid the tea in the library. Promptly at four I announced it was ready. With hands rubbing and rolling eyes the participants descended. Wasn't it fabulous? It was.

It was Iris who first noticed the dust. She fixed me with a reproachful eye. 'Honey, what's this?'

'It's a Georgian silver teaspoon.'

'Don't get cute. Look!' Her blood-red nail glowed dully in the surface of the offending implement. I bowed close and made an elaborate show of inspection. Boothby watched with care, ready to wade in. The thing baffled me. In the end I did the easiest thing and shook my head.

'It's *filthy*!'

Jayne Belle flung up her hands in horror. '*Aaaaaggghhh*!!'

Boothby Cunningham lifted his Royal Crown Derby cup with two fastidious fingers and examined it minutely. He tilted his head back and ran the fingers of his free hand through his hair. 'My *God*!'

Jayne Belle turned contorted features on me. Within her heaving bosom, life was still very far from being OK, despite the surrounding frenzy of activities. 'Mumsy's right. Paul, what the hell is *going on*?'

I was searching my mind for a suitable reply when her mother, who had put me in it, got me out of it.

'I hate to say this, honey,' Iris addressed her daughter with the same diplomacy as everyone else, 'but the whole house is full of it. I noticed it in my room.'

'*What*!! Paul, what's going on? Don't we have maids? I don't have to live like this!'

'I think you might have to for a while.'

Jayne Belle looked at her mother in horror. 'What! Why?'

'As long as all this work goes on there's going to be dust.'

'But that could be months!' Jayne Belle turned on Boothby and I shifted my feet in mild contentment. 'Boothby! How long is all this going to take?'

Boothby the artist stood his ground. His hands conducted an invisible symphony orchestra. 'You can't rush a project like this, you know.'

All this brought out the little girl in Jayne Belle. She stamped her foot and clenched her hands. 'Oh, what are we going to do? Mumsy. What are we going to *do*?'

Her mother watched her keenly. It was almost as if she had been preparing for this moment. 'We could always have a white Christmas.'

Boothby clutched his brow, 'My God! You don't mean you want me to paint the dust white?'

'I mean . . .' Iris paused dramatically. 'Philadelphia!'

— 8 —

Two days later we flew to the city made famous by W. C. Fields, and in which Thomas Jefferson had framed the American Constitution. In the limo from the airport the bravery and freedom were evenly distributed. Sitting upfront with the driver I myself felt neither. In the comfortable rear compartment it was fifty-fifty; Jayne Belle and her mother: brave and free. Denver and Tracey: definitely not. Following on behind in a cab with the large overflow of luggage was perhaps our least heroic member, Fong. Once I'd got the scenario through to him he had broken down into tormented and unintelligible gibberish. I didn't know what he was saying, but I knew what he meant.

Probably the free-est of all of us was Boothby Cunningham, three thousand miles away in Beverly Hills. Standing by the chuckling moat as he waved goodbye, almost all his languidness had deserted him. With his radiant smile he was positively animated.

It had been up to me to break the news to the parties, but not until I had voiced my own dismay. Wearily and without much hope I had plodded up the familiar stairs and knocked on the boudoir door.

'Who is it?'

'It's me, Paul.'

'What is it, Paul?'

'I need to speak to you.'

'What about?'

'About Christmas.'

At the mention of the magic word the door jerked open and Jayne Belle stood there, face flushed and eyes shining like a girl. 'Won't it be *fabulous*!'

'Well,' I looked at my feet for a moment, 'the thing is . . .'

Her face instantly darkened, 'What? What's the matter with you? Not sick?'

'No, no. It's just that . . .'

'Come on. Spit it out.'

I faced her bravely. 'I had been expecting to go home for Christmas.'

'Home? This is your home.'

'Of course, but . . .'

'What right have you to expect anything? On your salary it's *me* who's entitled to do all the expecting.'

'But my wife and children – '

'Get it straight, Paul. What your wife and kids need is your *job*. This is your family now. We *need* you here, and *you* need us. You're bought and paid for, see?'

I was beginning to.

'Now go tell Denver and Tracey and Fong to get packing. I can just about *hear* those jingle bells!'

Philadelphia was white, sure enough, in a greyish, rust-mottled way. The part of jingle bells was played by auto horns as the citizens battled through the grimy streets. The place was one huge snowdrift. The limo made painful progress through dismal brick suburbs, all very different from the endless bungalows of LA. These gave way to a ghettoish outskirt, full of diners advertising the world-famous Cheesesteak, the Philadelphia steak sandwich. We crossed a bridge and I caught a glimpse of the palladian temple steps ascended by Sylvester Stallone at the end of *Rocky*. Then we nosed into a wide avenue of department stores. The sidewalks were piled high with yellowing snow. Steam rose from gratings in the street, as in New York, but unlike New York each grating housed a freedom-loving inhabitant of the city which gave birth to the Dream. I looked out in wonder. I had never seen vagrancy on this scale, in such an uptown place. They camped openly at every corner, recent evacuees, I later learned, of the city's newly terminated madhouses. Clad in every sort of rag they clutched their wine in grimy hands and hassled indifferent passers-by for dimes.

Rittenhouse Square. *So* European! Reeks of old money. Snatches of the joyous chorus reached me, put up by Iris and Jayne Belle. I wondered if it had some genealogical connection to Jimmy. His money was certainly old. No member of his family had lifted a finger for at least two generations.

The old-world, grey-stone square was built around a large central garden which was well tended and vagrant-free. One or two modern blocks had crept in, and one or two smart, glass storefronts.

Our hotel, the Grosvenor, had been carefully protected from the ravages of modernisation. The dull gold sign, laid large along the entire second floor, reminded me of the grand old railway hotels of midlands England. It boasted a narrow, wooden porch complete with revolving door, and a green mat inscribed in well-trodden letters with its name.

As we approached, Jayne Belle's excitement got the better of her. Pulling a protesting Tracey out of the way she knelt on her back-facing dickey seat and slid back the glass division.

'Paul, honey, you *did* book?!'

'Of course I booked.' I was beginning to feel extremely disorientated in this strange place.

'The *best* suite?'

'The absolute best. And another for your mother adjoining.'

'Fabulous! And my husband doesn't know a thing?'

'Not a thing.'

It had been Iris's idea to surprise Kenny. I couldn't help wondering just how thrilled he was going to be. Although on the surface all the talk between the ladies had been of Peace and Goodwill to All Men, I suspected an undercurrent. Sammy Peach, after all, father of one and ex-husband of the other, was mixed up in this. Sammy, who had so signally failed as a husband and father, and after thirty-six years of marriage. Who could say that Kenny, in the corruptive ambience of his ex-father-in-law, might not also skid off the rails? That this might lead to a case of like mother like daughter, that it was somehow inevitable – this was the undercurrent. Men cannot be left on the loose for long without getting into trouble. Particularly important men with plenty of cash on movie sets. They are, as Iris often said, animals.

Another important man, a most important-*looking* man, greeted us profusely in the lobby of the Grosvenor Hotel. We'd got through the revolving door, just about, and were trying to get our bearings in the dim atmosphere, when he materialised, from behind an aspidistra. What he lacked in height he made up for in old-world diablerie. He wore an orchid in the buttonhole of his morning coat. He clapped and bowed. 'Good *morning*, ladies. Good morning, good morning, good morning!'

When he bowed he presented a highly polished pink dome, black strands elaborately plastered on either side of it. When he clapped he clapped lavender-gloved hands. 'And how was your journey? Not too fatiguing, I trust?' When he spoke his reptilian features writhed with extreme mobility. The red mouth, with its full lower lip, curved in a glory of unctuousness, taking up, when he smiled, almost the whole of his lower face.

The ladies looked at each other and stroked their minks. This was it, surely? In the Grosvenor Hotel, Rittenhouse Square, Philadelphia, the age of chivalry was indeed not dead.

Jayne Belle, in her most refined voice, said, 'I am Mrs Graumann and this is my mother, Mrs Peach. We have reservations, I believe?'

'Of course!' The welcomer bowed and clapped more vigorously than ever. 'Of course, of course! Delighted! I am the manager. My name is Wilberforce.'

'Mr Wilberforce.' Jayne Belle fingered one pearl-and-emerald earring. 'How charming.'

More clapping produced two pages, one very old and white, the other very young and black. Their uniforms were identical, both made, apparently, for someone else. They had tiny brass buttons all down their fronts, and pill-box hats. For all their oppositeness both seemed equally keen to convey that neither were really like this, in real life. They were directed imperiously by Mr Wilberforce to assist with the bags. Jayne Belle said, not to be outdone in imperiousness, 'Paul, help them, show them. Where the *hell* is Fong?'

Fong was still in the smoke-filled cab, looking dazed. I suppose he thought that if he postponed entering the hotel for long enough he might become forgotten in the excitement. Between us and the pages, we somehow managed the party and its mountain of baggage, up to the twentieth floor. The Grosvenor operated two elevators only, built like upended wooden coffins, which climbed, groaning, at a snail's pace.

The twentieth floor boasted the penthouse suite, reserved with the greatest of pleasure for Mrs Graumann.

Tracey and Denver refused to share a room and got in a fight, first with each other, then with their mom. Jayne Belle was too tired to argue. At first it looked as though Fong and I would have to share, to accommodate them. Then another room was found, but not on the same floor. Would that suffice? It would suffice for Fong but not for Paul. Paul was needed to be near at hand at all times. Fong nodded hard. For once he seemed to understand perfectly.

Mr Kenny Graumann, it transpired, was not in his modest room on the sixth floor, but was expected back later. The ladies retired to their suites to rest. I made it to my room and locked the door. It had a colour TV and a mini-bar with all manner of miniaturised wines and spirits. I transferred a quantity to a glass, found a movie, lay on the bed. I thought: what the hell.

*

I was jerked awake by the bedside phone.

'Where *are* you?'

'Must've dropped off, I guess.'

'Drop on again, dammit! My husband needs you in here *now*.'

'Is he enjoying his surprise?'

'Don't get cute, honey. This is not the time.'

The suite was bright yellow and blue. I caught a glimpse of pink bath tiles through an open door. Jayne Belle reclined on a yellow sofa, looking dangerous. Kenny paced up and down in his shirtsleeves. 'How should I know where your father is? Am I his keeper already? Somewheres in New York. He can afford those prices! Ay ay ay!'

Jayne Belle's eyes narrowed suspiciously. 'This place is cheap?'

'It was till you arrived. Ya got any idea what all this is costing?' He waved his arms tormentedly at the accommodation.

Jayne Belle glared at me.

'And Fong. Why do we need Fong, fer Chrissakes? The hotel doesn't have kitchens?'

'It's *Christmas*, honey.'

'So?'

'I plan to have a *fabulous* Christmas party. Roasted turkey! Mince pies!'

'Every goddam store in town is selling mince pies.'

'Not like Fong makes 'em. And his roasted turkey! Mmmmm.'

'And where's he gonna cook all this stuff?'

'In the hotel kitchens, of course.'

'Do they know?'

'Paul will arrange it all, won't you honey?' She gave me a dazzling smile.

Kenny became aware of me for the first time. He gave me an accusing look. I wondered nervously what portion of blame was to be meted out to me.

'You wanted me, Sir?'

'There's no pumpernickel bagels in this town.'

'I shall attend to it immediately, Sir.'
'Good. You do that.'

By breakfast time I had tracked down the bagels and was able to serve them, thinly sliced and toasted just the way Kenny like them, in the suite. They were a little pale, but . . . Kenny shrugged in martyred resignation.

This morning, however, bagels were not the biggest problem. Jayne Belle was locked in the bathroom, very upset.

'Is there anything I can do, Sir?' I enquired, Admirable Crighton to my fingertips.

'She doesn't like the decor.'

'I *hate* it!' Her anguished voice filtered through the woodwork. Kenny raised his hands, palm up, to heaven. 'You better call Boothby, I guess.'

Another suite was concocted on the twentieth floor by Mr Wilberforce. Other guests, suddenly less important, were prised from adjoining rooms. Furniture was rearranged. Wilberforce directed the pages with much panache. The result, however alluring, did little to please Boothby. He arrived, shagged and moody, toting his Gucci bags, a shadow of the carefree creature so recently seen waving in the California sun.

Jayne Belle was impervious to his distress. 'Let's go to work! We've barely a week.'

The decorative theme in Jayne Belle's enlarged suite was to be European Christmas Past. The name of Charles Dickens was brought into play, as Jayne Belle's energies were focused, like laser beams.

Her mother offered clues from her considerable, if dim, experience of the Pennsylvania Main Line, where Old Money and all things old hold sway. Boothby was able, with relative impunity, to show contempt for Iris's views, which cheered him up slightly.

Clarence Wilberforce (Boothby's arrival inspired first-name terms) was swept along by the tide of events. It was all most irregular, most. The words oozed from his damp lips, his hands writhed in ecstasy. Mrs Graumann had undertaken to foot all bills for conversion to, and restoration from, her vision of Christmas Past.

Minions with ladders and pots and fabrics and paper and every sort of fixture and fitting that Philadelphia could offer, were cajoled and chivvied by Clarence Wilberforce, in and out of Jayne Belle's presence. Charles Dickens, I couldn't help reflecting, would probably have liked him.

Kenny, unable to stand it any longer, retreated to his mysterious movie set in New York and was rarely seen. In Jayne Belle's intensely creative frame of mind he was rarely missed.

For those of us remaining it was exhausting work. Many of the minutiae of a fabulous and authentic English Christmas had to be hunted down, and who could be better suited to the task than an English butler like me? By night I was usually too tired for sleep. One day melted painfully into another, as the exhaustion compounded.

One night I lay there tossing fitfully in the flickering light from the TV. I looked for the fiftieth time at the digital clock: 0436. I was reaching for yet another sip of water when the telephone rang. I was shocked but not surprised. Expecting Jayne Belle I picked it up. The line hummed and hissed emptily. My nerves contracted at the idea of long distance. I said, guardedly, 'Hallo?'

'Hallo?' The voice sounded far away. 'Dad?'

'Olly?' I was listening to hear the voice of my oldest son. He said, 'What time is it?'

'Late. Don't worry.'

'Sorry Dad. I couldn't work it out. I didn't want anyone to hear me.'

'Is something wrong?' I felt my throat closing up.

'I think you should come home, Dad,' his thirteen-year-old voice croaked earnestly.

'I wish I could.'

'You mean you're not? It's Christmas.'

'Don't I know it.'

'Surely you get time off for Christmas?'

I had been meaning to ring and tell them. Something had always got in the way. Things back home seemed easier if they were not faced.

''Fraid not.' I laughed hollowly. It echoed back at me.

'The thing is, Dad . . .' The boy's voice paused uncertainly. 'I'm awfully worried about Mum.'

'What's wrong?' My tension turned to a cold and ringing calm.

'I don't know. She seems awfully upset. I think it's something to do with Nigel . . .'

'Is he being awful to her? I'll kill him!'

'I don't know. I think you should come home, that's all. I think she needs you.'

'What sort of upset is she?'

'I don't know. She cries a lot. *Please*, Dad.'

'Olly, I *can't*. Not quite yet, anyway.'

'Granny's being awful to her. Granny *is* awful.'

'Look, Olly, I can't get back before Christmas. You can't imagine what it's like here. Tell Mum I love her and I'll call on Christmas Day.'

There was a pause on the line, like a sigh.'

'Olly? I love you. I love you all. Very much.'

'Yeah, Dad, OK. 'Bye.'

And it was over. I lay on the bed, the telephone still cradled to my ear, almost levitating with cold aftershock. The hotel operator came onto the line. In a sleepy voice he said, 'Are you all through?'

'Yes,' I replied. 'I'm all through.'

Christmas Eve. The suite glowed and twinkled. The huge tree, decorated by Boothby, groaned beneath the weight of genuine Victorian ornaments garnered by him from the many antique shops in town. Tonight was party night: a sit-down affair for family and friends and selected celebrity guests. These included Victor Ventura, who had a small part in Kenny's movie. The star turn, however, had been procured by Boothby.

The Harmsworth Hossenffeffers were the oldest money in town. Saxon chieftains by blood, in the nineteenth century the Hossenffeffers had brought whisky and railroads to the American West. When it came to European manners and culture, well, Harmsworth was just about the last word in it. He had been educated there to such an extent, there was almost nothing American about him. Eton, Oxford, the Sorbonne – he exuded it. He spent much of his time there, owned castles in Scotland and Ireland, a chateau on the Loire. And what he didn't leave he had carted back with him to Rittenhouse Square. The Hossenffeffer mansion stood opposite, its crumbling exterior guarding one of the world's great art collections.

All this we learnt from Boothby. He tossed off the information in a languid, uninterested way, almost on the point of fainting from the sheer ennui of it. Jayne Belle's eyes shone. Boothby's stock had never been higher. To have snagged such a social marlin. The biggest! And on Christmas Eve! She rubbed her hands and yet again went over the placements at the groaning table. Now, Harmsworth would sit on her right . . .

The feast rested in the hands of myself and Fong. A pantry had been set up in yet another adjoining room, equipped with hot-plates, warmers, fridges and silver serving trays. I had amassed a large number of bottles, which was all to the good. Fong was introduced into the subterranean world of the hotel kitchens. The head chef was a huge German. He didn't seem to like the arrangement much. Neither did Fong. But such was the charisma of Clarence Wilberforce that an armed truce prevailed.

I was snatching a few moments to myself in my room that afternoon when there was a soft tap at my door.

'Come in,' I said, as discouragingly as I could. I was surprised to see the angular features of Fong. Even more surprising, they were contorted into a lopsided smile. 'Me talkee you?' The smile enlarged.

'Sure,' I said, also smiling.

'You vey good boy.'

'Oh?'

'Missee likee you. You Number One!'

I shook my head modestly. 'Number Nine.' We both laughed.

'You helpee me, maybe.'

'If I can.' I shot my cuffs in a Number One sort of way.

'You talkee Missee me.'

'Oh, yes?' I said, becoming guarded.

'Me go home California.'

'What? Not today! No way!'

'Ayee. No way!' Fong's face cracked open even wider, baring his brown teeth. 'No today. Soon. Vey soon.'

'Gosh, I don't know. What shall I say?'

'You no say Missee. Me tell you. You good boy.'

'What is it? What's the problem?'

'Tenants no pay. Vey *bad*.'

I remembered the line of shufflers the night of the Domingo dinner. 'I've never really understood . . .'

Fong smiled craftily. 'You no worry you. Me workee workee. Makee money. Bling family Amelica. Apartment housees. Now no good. People no pay.'

'I see.'

'You good boy. You helpee me, me helpee you.'

'OK, Fong,' I said, glad at least to be cordial. 'I'll see what I can do.'

The interview over, Fong moved swiftly to the door. As he passed through it he turned and raised a blackened thumb at me, 'Number *One*!'

Kenny, struggling into the velvet jacket while I hovered about the suite making last-minute adjustments, was disparaging about the Hossenffeffers.

'I thought this was a family dinner. Family and friends.'

'You call that horrible Victor a friend?' Jayne Belle, intent at her mirror, halfway round her mouth with a lipstick, paused to parry venomously.

'Of course he's a friend. A very old friend. We got the same heart surgeon even.'

'He hates you.'

'How could he hate me? I just gave him a part in my movie arready.'

'A bit-part. That's why he hates you.'

'That doesn't alter the fact I don't know this putz Huffenstuff from a crock o' shit.'

'Everybody hates you, you shmuck. You don't know from *nothin'*. You should be *proud*. Don't you *understand*? Don't you understand *anything*? It's an *honour* they should come to our party!'

'I should be proud to know some bum with lotta bucks he never had ta woik for?'

'You animal! Don't you understand *anything* about art? About culture?'

'Art costs. That's all I know from art.'

The discussion was saved from further deterioration by a discreet tapping at the door. I padded over and opened it. Clarence Wilberforce stood without, the radiant centrepiece in a semi-circle of youngish females dressed in mob-caps and crinolines. He described a series of elaborate figures in the air with his lavendar gloves. 'May I have the honour of presenting . . . the Merrywoode Singers!'

At the mention of this name Jayne Belle abandoned her face and came dancing across the suite.

'Oh, Mr Wilberforce! You managed it! Oh, how *fabulous*!'

'Managed what already?' This was a surprise. I was surprised, but not as surprised as Kenny. He stood with his mouth open as the songstresses filed in.

What Mr Wilberforce had managed, against all the odds, and at impossible notice, was the crowning glory Jayne Belle had dreamed of, in honour of the Hossenffeffers. In deference to their assumed Christianity, and in the true spirit of Christmas, the Merrywoode Singers would arrange themselves in some convenient corner of the suite. Then, at whatever intervals seemed appropriate, they would sing a selection of Christmas carols throughout the course of the evening.

Iris, attracted by the commotion, arrived on the scene, blazing with jewels. She wore a low-cut evening gown of aubergine satin.

Jayne Belle squeaked, 'Mother! Rubies!'

'So?'

'I was going to wear rubies. I told you.'

'You told me diamonds.'

'Rubies look so fabulous, so Christmassy. Couldn't we both wear rubies?'

'Sure, honey.'

'We won't clash?'

I cleared my throat. 'Ladies . . .'

'What is it?' They both turned on me.

'Might I suggest that we position the carollers in the alcove?'

The ladies bustled over to assist with the stage management. The next few minutes were hectic, for all of us except Kenny. At last it was time for a run-through. The Merrywoode Singers raised their voices: 'Once in Royal David's city, Stood a lonely ca-a-ttle shed . . .'

Kenny hurried from the room, his hands over his ears.

Other guests trickled in: Boothby, in a raspberry tuxedo and Regency ruffled shirt. Tracey, dark and demure in blue. Denver, writhing with discomfort in his bar-mitzvah blazer and black shiny shoes. Victor Ventura made his entrance with all the drama at his disposal. His usual lady companion hovered smiling in the background, somehow, by her modesty, proclaiming his immortal fame. His own proclamations were less understated. One would have thought the Merrywoode Singers had been hired merely as a backdrop for his performance. Instantly recognising their potential, it was the work of a moment for the star to position himself strategically before them. 'Ya know "O Sole Mio"?'

The leading Merrywoode nodded her blonde bangs, her eyes bright with recognition of an idol of her not-so-recent youth. Victor tore the nautical cap from the bronze luxuriance of his wig and belted into the song, very much in the manner of Placido Domingo, until the chandeliers rattled. When the final high-note gave way to a room full of fulsome appreciation he stepped into the throng and put his arm lovingly around my shoulders.

'Well, old boy . . .' His English accent was pure Terry Thomas. 'What've you got for us tonight?'

I had got mulled claret, spiced with cinnamon. My own insides had been warmed by it during recent and exhaustive tests in my makeshift pantry. I passed it around with the assistance of two elderly waiters seconded for the evening by Clarence from the hotel dining room. Ding dong merrily on high was the desired effect. Even Denver cheered up, and Kenny seemed better able to blot out the carols.

Christmas cheer filled the room when the last but not the least of Jayne Belle's guests made their belated appearance. Clarence Wilberforce ushered in the Harmsworth Hossenffeffers, his every gesture humbly heralding the arrival of royalty. A hush descended as the awful magnitude of so much unearned income dawned on us. Mr and Mrs Harmsworth Hossenffeffer, on first sighting, had the disturbing appearance of twins, two sides of one rare and ancient coin. Both were tall, spare, stooped, imposing. Both had cropped, white hair and pink, bony faces. Both had eyes of pale quizzical blue, swimming in pink; eyes that, while they might have endured inconvenience, had never suffered hardship.

Not only were the Harmsworth Hossenffeffers possessed of the oldest money in town, and perhaps the oldest bodies, they wore the oldest clothes. Harmsworth Hossenffeffer's immaculate black dinner jacket was turning green with age. Mrs Harmsworth Hossenffeffer wore a black dress which might, at one time, have been wool. A tiny diamond brooch at the shoulder was her only concession to wealth. I was standing next to Iris and I heard her murmur, 'My God! You can almost smell the mothballs.'

There was another disturbing thing about the Harmsworth Hossenffeffers, it didn't take me long to realise. They knew how to carry it off with dignity, but to my trained eye there was no doubt: they were both as drunk as lords.

The party was seated graciously by Jayne Belle. Harmsworth Hossenffeffer sat on her right, as she had dreamed of. Mrs Harmsworth Hossenffeffer was positioned further down the table, next to Victor Ventura. Something about this arrangement seemed to displease Harmsworth Hossenffeffer. He bent a disquieting stare upon the actor, frowning silently, then suddenly exclaimed in a high-Anglican tremolo, 'I know you!'

Victor Ventura smirked uncertainly.

'Saw you in a motion picture once. Long time ago.'

Jayne Belle placed jewelled fingers on the extreme edge of her guest-of-honour's mildewed cuff. 'That is Victor Ventura, the famous movie star.'

Harmsworth Hossenffeffer snorted. 'Don't approve of motion pictures. Popular culture, particularly American popular culture, is the greatest danger facing civilisation today.'

I started to duck in and out of the dinner party conversations. Victor Ventura was laughing at his own jokes. He had managed to work the conversation around to the subject of acting. I could see at a glance it was a topic in which the Harmsworth Hossenffeffers felt unable to join. They sat like statues, drinking steadily and staring into space. The rest of us were free to share in great moments remembered from the Actors Studio with Lee and Marlon: 'We had ta be able ta play any part – *any* part,' Victor paused with pointing finger and staring eye. 'At the drop of a hat. And *be* that person!'

'Go on then,' the challenge came unexpectedly from Tracey. She flushed when the attention switched to her, her hot cheeks downy and childish. 'I mean, show us, ya know, *be* someone now.'

Victor Ventura, on the spot, was not the man to pass up an

opportunity. Centre stage was where he liked to be, and any audience would do, even one which included the Harmsworth Hossenffeffers.

The dramatic eye swept the room. Some sixth sense warned me, but it was too late. Perhaps my very rigidity betrayed me. Victor Ventura, I instinctively knew, was too old a pro to miss a role so steeped in potential for hamming it up. What great artist has not played the Butler, after all? Our eyes met. Victor smiled, as a man might do while sighting his gun at a sitting bird. 'Paul. You're not such a bad actor yourself. Tell ya what. You be me, and I'll be you.'

Reaction to this suggestion was mixed. Jayne Belle and I, for once in accord, registered horror; most of the rest, unstinted enthusiasm. The Harmsworth Hossenffeffers registered nothing.

The majority won the day, swept along on the unstoppable tide of Victor, and I found myself, almost before I knew it, clad in his tight reefer jacket, stripped of the reassurance of my salt-and-pepper tie, sitting next to Mrs Harmsworth Hossenffeffer.

Once he got my silver tray in his hands there was no stopping the old thespian. Almost doubled up with servility he pranced and grovelled about the room, a liveried Quasimodo.

'Yes, Sir,' he crawled. 'No, Madam,' he whined.

Mrs Harmsworth Hossenffeffer turned dismissively from the hilarity of these vulgar antics, and focused her watery gaze on me.

'I detect that you are English.'

'Absolutely!' I was not at all at home, sitting down, even in Victor's jacket. I welcomed the fact that she was a stranger, and her veiled suggestion of affinity. The idea that she was possibly senile and almost certainly plastered conspired to relax me further.

'Educated, from the sound of it.' Her 's' was slightly slurred.

'At great expense,' I quipped, more at home by the moment.

Mrs Harmsworth Hossenffeffer supped her wine reflectively,

her eyes empty on my face, her bloodless lips stained in the corners with purple.

'How do you stand it?'

'I'm sorry. I don't quite follow.' The bell warning me of the possible approach of the spectre of divided loyalties, sounded clearly enough, but nothing could have prepared me for her next observation. Raising her voice so it could be heard clearly above the din of Victor's audience, she said, 'These bloody Jews, always whining on about the alleged holocaust.' I gaped at her, spellbound. The horrible hush that fell only paved the way for what she had to say next. Raising her glass in the general direction of the Christmas tree she continued, 'After all, who was it killed Jesus, anyway?' No one had an answer to this, least of all me. In the calm before the storm, in the still, small voice after the rushing, mighty wind of Jehovah, I caught Kenny's cold, unwinking eye. It was fixed on me. Through all the injustice I could feel his blame eating into me.

Not knowing what to do, or what I was doing, I sprang away from the table, away from the contamination of my partner, knocking over my chair. The noise of it seemed surreal. Everything was in slow motion. Victor Ventura was frozen and speechless. I realised that I was heading instinctively for the Merrywoode Singers. Out of the corner of my eye I saw Tracey and Denver leaving the table as well, heading for the door, hot with honest childish anger. I addressed the Merrywoode Singers. There was a commanding urgency in my voice.

'Sing,' I ordered. 'Sing your hearts out!'

'What would you like?' said the leader. There was panic in her eye.

'Anything. Something loud.'

My desperation seemed to pull her together. She made her choice and briskly instructed the others. In the circumstances it might not have been the wisest, but it was the loudest. They raised their voices to heaven and roared, *'O Come All Ye Faithful, Joyful and Triumphant . . .'*

I bolted back to the pantry.

Almost immediately, I returned, surprised by the strength of my feeling of outrage. I felt profoundly protective towards my adoptive family. They seemed small and helpless, somehow, against the slings and arrows of a Goliathan world, despite their wealth. I bore turkey to them like an offering.

Victor Ventura had resumed his seat, the joke over. Next to him Mrs Harmsworth Hossenffeffer appeared to have fallen asleep. Her husband was blithely engaged in conversation with a flustered Boothby on the subject of early Etruscan art. Kenny had disappeared. The Merrywoode Singers were in between numbers.

When Harmsworth Hossenffeffer fell briefly silent on the subject of the Etruscans, Jayne Belle tackled him brightly. You could see she had made up her mind that nothing unpleasant should spoil her party.

'Mr Hossenffeffer,' she cooed, 'surely you have a favourite Christmas carol you'd like our choristers to sing?'

'Why, yes.' His parchment skin crumpled in pleasure as he bared his yellow fangs. 'Something we always sing in Milliece, *"Lumière du monde nous adorons"*, you know that one?' He squinted astringently at the Merrywoodes.

I could see from the crestfallen look on their faces, reflected on those of Iris and Jayne Belle, that Harmsworth Hossenffeffer's request did not feature in their current repertoire.

The general dismay was eclipsed, however, by the unscheduled sound of vigorous strumming on an acoustic guitar. It came from outside the door, which soon opened, revealing the source to be Denver. He wore an embroidered skullcap and had taken off his tie. Jayne Belle gave a small shriek, which was drowned by the music.

Denver was accompanied by his sister. She wore a shawl over her head, her dark eyes glowing to the melody of 'Hava Nagila', played slow.

As the tempo of the ancient song increased, the third member of the troupe came whirling into the room. Kenny, too, had discarded his tie, and the cossack legs he worked so furiously, regardless of the condition of the heart that pumped them, were encased in screaming tartan trews.

Not long after this the Harmsworth Hossenffeffers left, without bothering to sample Fong's renowned mince pies.

Christmas morning. I was woken by a knock on my door. 'Merry Christmas, Sir!'

It was Elmer, the older page. He was bearing gifts. He came over to the bed and dumped them there. I sat up and rubbed my eyes. 'What's all this?'

'Compliments of the Season from the Grosvenor Hotel.' Elmer made it sound like a funeral oration. He indicated something bottle-shaped, tightly wrapped, with a highly professional pink bow at the neck.

'Don't worry,' he added mournfully, 'we all get them.'

'What's the other one?'

'How should I know?' Elmer looked hurt and resentful. 'Sump'n from your bosses.'

I tore at the wrapping and he stood by the bed watching, gloomier by the moment. 'One thing about being a domestic,' Elmer sighed, almost drowning in pathos, 'you always get remembered at Christmas.'

We both stared down dully at my gift, me and my soupstained Santa. Elmer scratched the pink back of his head, pushing his pillbox hat forward.

'What in tarnation is *that*?'

It was a ball of fine metal wires, stuck on the end of a black plastic stalk, with a black plastic base. I examined it from all angles, trying to detect its purpose. I found batteries fitted beneath, and a red switch. I pushed the switch and the ball revolved slowly. The shiny spines caught the light, producing faint rainbows. I looked up at Elmer. We both shrugged, none the wiser. There was a card, illustrated in one corner with bells and holly. I deciphered Jayne Belle's biro scrawl:

Merry Xmas, honey! Just a little something for your room.

*We're going out, so take the day off. You deserve it. Love, Mr
and Mrs Graumann and Family. XXX*

I spent Christmas morning in my room, not quite sure what
to do with all the unaccustomed free time. I wasn't used to not
being on the go. I felt guilty. I had a hot bath, trying to relax,
but after five minutes it was over. I ordered and consumed a
lavish, room-service breakfast, culminating in flatulence and
depression. There were small bottles of champagne in the
mini-bar. I thought about them as I flicked around the channels
on my big hotel TV. After all, it *was* Christmas. After a while
I drank one. The depression increased.

They would have finished Christmas lunch at home. The
thought made me nervous and sad. I drank another mini-
champagne, sitting on the bed, and stared apprehensively at
the phone.

The ringing tone went on even longer than usual. I had
plenty of time to imagine laughter around the tree, wrapping
paper littering the Great Hall of Lady Roxbury's shabbily
exquisite manor house. In my mind's eye I saw the reluctant drag of feet away from the fireside's festive glow, to
traipse down the long stone passage and answer the blasted
phone.

'Hallo?'

'Natasha?' The line was lousy.

'Is that you, Nigel?'

'No, Millie, it's Paul.'

'Oh, 'allo Paul. Merry Christmas. Do they 'ave Christmas
over there?'

'Sort of. Is everybody merry over there?'

'I think so, dear. They're not 'ere.'

'Not there?'

'They've all gorn over to Mister Nigel's. 'E's laid on a right
smashing blow-out by all accounts.'

My flatulence and depression achieved a new low. 'When
will they be back?'

'I dunno, dear. I think there's going to be dancing. You know what Lady R is for dancing 'til dawn. They'll maybe all sleep over there.'

'Oh, well. You'll let them know I rang, won't you? Say I said "Merry Christmas".'

'And the same to you, luvvie.'

'Bye bye, Millie.'

'Bye bye.'

The line and I went dead. I hung up and resumed my staring at the instrument of so much disappointment and heartache.

I was startled when it squawked into life; even more so when I heard who it was: 'Now is the winter of our discontent made *glorious* summer . . . how are ya fixed for Christmas lunch?'

'Mr Ventura!'

'Call me Victor, *please*! Now, whaddya say?'

'You mean you're inviting me?'

'*Sure* I'm invitin' ya. Ya need a printed invitation?'

'No, no. That's very kind. I'm not doing anything.'

'Meet me in the bar in five.'

'I've only got my butler clothes, I'm afraid.'

'So much the better.'

Grand Echezaux goes down well with plum pudding. Clarence Wilberforce, extra-resplendent on Christmas day, had disputed it, preferring to recommend port, but he gave in with elaborate deference to a star of such albeit waning radiance as Victor Ventura. It had gone down well with the preceding goose. Before that Le Montrachet had gone down well with the oysters. Before them the very dry martinis had gone down well on their own.

We were at the Stilton stage. Clarence had dug up some *very* old brandy, not unlike the stuff I'd paid through the nose for on the beach all those lifetimes ago. All this splendour down the hatch and I was still in the dark about Vic's (as I now called him) motives, if not about many magic moments in his long career.

He got into it, when he thought the time was right, with

startling directness. 'So, Paul, my friend, tell me frankly . . .' His blue eyes twinkled shrewdly and his complexion glowed, almost matching his bronze thatch. 'Whaddya think of your boss?'

My system sounded the alarm, even through the haze of Christmas cheer. Seeing the look on my face Victor added, 'He's my boss too, ya know, right now.'

'You've got a part in his movie, haven't you?' I felt relief at steering into what looked like friendlier waters. They weren't. Victor's face darkened.

'You call that a *part*?'

'I don't know, I – '

'You know what I call it?' Victor's face was a mask of anger. 'I call it an *insult*.'

'Oh, dear.'

'As one performer to another, Paul,' Victor took an emotional pull at his snifter, 'it's a *goddam* insult!'

I was lost for words. He continued, 'So ya wanna know what I think of your boss?'

I didn't think I did, but there was no stopping Victor Ventura. 'He's a cheap two-bit shmuck makin' shlock pictures fulla schwartzers.'

I dived for cover into my glass, but by now my responses didn't matter to my host. He was off and running, blinded by the arclights of his mind.

'But I got it all figured out, see? I got it figured how we can get back at the cheap bastard.'

'We?'

'Yes, Paul,' he said, reaching across and placing a warm, pudgy manacle over my wrist, '*we*.'

'I'm afraid I don't understand.'

'Listen ta me and ya will. Last night it came ta me in a flash.' His face had taken on a rapturous, musing look. 'The Movie of a Lifetime.'

'Movie? What movie?'

'At dinner when I traded places with ya. I knew it was *the* role, made in heaven just for me, Victor Ventura . . .' His eyes half-closed dreamily, his hands conducted unseen orchestras. 'I see the marquee now . . . "The Admirable Victor"!'

I said, 'You mean . . .?' But Victor continued.

'What great actor has not played the Butler role? Laughton, Barrymore . . .' Suddenly he jerked himself back to earth and became animated. 'And there's a *great* part for *you*, Paul. A *great* part!'

'But I'm not an actor!'

'Not an actor!' Victor Ventura sat back in his chair as if stunned. He regarded me with frank astonishment, sizing me up with his hands like a prize pig. 'Not an *actor*? Gimme a *break*! Not only that . . .' (Here his face became wily as he leaned across the table to confide) '. . . you're the story consultant on the picture.'

'This is definite, is it? I mean, it's a definite thing?'

'When Victor Ventura says "let's go" on a project, it's *definite*!'

'That's pretty exciting.'

'Sure it's exciting. All ya gotta do is spill the beans.'

'How d'you mean?'

'Here, maybe this'll help ya.' Victor produced a small black object, about the size of a prayer-book. 'This is how it woiks, see? Put this in your pocket. Then this here,' he held up a black button on the end of a wire, 'ya put this in your buttonhole, hidden in a flower or sump'n.'

'You mean it's a tape recorder?' Through the haze I felt a cold hand grip my guts.

'Right, kid.'

'You want me to spy on the Graumanns?'

'Right again. I want every detail of their no-good life. That's the meat on the bone of this project. We'll fix those cheap bastards.' His face had become a shrunken head of meanness.

With the clarity that sometimes comes with wine, all the ugliness of this embittered thespian was revealed to me. Also with the wine came rage. I felt myself rising uncontrollably from the table, recoiling from contamination. I felt as I had the night before when they were under attack. I shared a life with my employers. They were my protectors and, damn it, I was theirs. I felt as protective as a lion with its young. They were vulnerable, and I would *never* let them down.

I hurled my napkin to the table. 'An *outrage* . . .' I could hear my voice, clear and cold. Other lunchers heard it to. Curious faces swam up at me, out of a seasick sea. I caught a queasy glimpse of a flustered Clarence approaching. '. . . A *bloody* outrage. You bloody people. You just don't have a clue about the meaning of True Blue . . .' The booze was whipping up the words into a self-perpetuating crescendo. Rage had subverted reason. My mood, however spurious or real, had a life of its own. All the frustration of the past year had at last found an outlet. I picked up the table and made to tip it onto the ageing star.

'*Hey*!' The jaunty cap and youthful hair slid together over one ear. 'I gotta heart condition!'

'You haven't even got a *heart*!' Something attached itself to my arm as I bellowed these words. It was Clarence. I didn't realise until I'd sent him sprawling to the floor. The sight of him there had a sobering effect.

'Mr Wilberforce! I say, I'm awfully sorry . . .'

He picked himself up, examining and adjusting his parts professionally. He was unflappably calm. His manner reminded me of my own uniform. 'You'd better go.'

I bowed slightly. 'Perhaps you're right.'

'I know I'm right.'

From within the debris came the well-trained voice of Victor Ventura, 'Goddam limeys! Can't hold their goddam liquor.'

Clarence pursed his lips. 'Let's hope folks hold their tongues, so your employers don't get to hear about this.'

In the dead time of Boxing Day the spirit of goodwill withered and died in the bosom of Jayne Belle. Kenny had fled back to New York and his mysterious movie location. Her mother had the toothache. Jayne Belle had cabin fever. She was very upset.

She summoned me to her suite. 'Paul, I'm very upset.' Her face had that gaunt, leathery look, like a giant lizard cheated of its prey. I assumed she must have heard about the goings-on in the hotel dining room.

'Denver and Tracey will have to go home.'

So that was it. I was relieved not to be the immediate source of her distress, though I knew how close I was to becoming the victim of it.

Tracey and Denver were at the root of her humiliation before the Harmsworth Hossenffeffers. In her heart that much had become indisputable. No further social progress could be made on the Main Line with them around. But how could it be done? That's what she wanted me to tell her. Alone in Beverly Hills, unsupervised, who knew what damage those two rebels might wreak?

Despite the mental numbness which Jayne Belle in this mood unfailingly induced, I was able to provide her with a hot suggestion.

'Why can't Fong go with them?'

She gave me her deadliest look. The idea was good enough to make her angrier than ever. Her eyes were bright and hard. 'It'll mean more *work* for you.'

'That's OK.'

'It *better* be.'

Denver and Tracey were thrilled when I broke the news, but not as thrilled as Fong.

'You *vey* good boy.' In his room on the floor below, the smell of Chinese cooking was overpowering. His rice machine stood on the hotel writing table, steaming away.

I shrugged and smiled. 'Anything to oblige.'

'You talkee good. No good all the time "missee missee missee".'

'I couldn't agree more. Absolutely!'

— 164 —

'You richee guy.'

'Hardly!'

'Sure. You richee guy. Richee guy no money no good.'

'I heard that!'

'Here.' Before I knew what was happening, he'd pushed a thick, dirty envelope into my hand. 'You good boy. Number One.'

I looked down at the wad, back up at Fong. 'I can't possibly accept this!'

'Good for you. Good for you *wife*.'

I pondered on this. 'But . . .'

'No but. You no takee, me vey *angly*!' Fong made his more familiar 'angry' face. We both laughed.

I shoved the money in my pocket. 'I wouldn't want that!'

We shook hands warmly and said goodbye.

Back in my room I counted the mixed bag of grimy bills. It added up to a grand.

— 9 —

The days dragged by, and nothing about Philadelphia made them any rosier. The snow persisted, deep and dirty and hard. Jayne Belle and Iris discovered more and more things, familiar in Beverly Hills, that couldn't be found in this city, and packed me off daily to find them. Each quest was harder and sillier than the last, each disappointment keener.

One morning I was in the lobby, discussing with the desk clerk the remote possibility of there being a willcall zen foot reflexologist in town, when a minor commotion by the revolving doors distracted me.

Clarence Wilberforce, in full regalia, was discreetly quizzing a suspect caller. The suspect caller, less discreet, was Doctor Love.

'But how . . .?' I didn't understand it.

'Tracked you down through Denver.'

'Ah. But why?' We were lounging in some high-backed armchairs, usually the preserve of genteel coffee-sippers. Clarence himself had seated us, behind his largest aspidistra. He kept glancing over, not sure if we were sufficiently hidden. Doctor Love had embroidered some bright new love-beads onto his denim cap, and carried his monstrous ghetto-blaster. Clarence wasn't sure, you could tell, when that ghetto-blaster was going to start blasting.

'Why I'm here is *heavy*, British.' Love looked owlish.

'Heavy?'

'Sump'n' goin' on in New York you gotta see, right *NOW*.'

From the fug of a converted Victorian landaulette I smirked out at Love as I ran my scam past Iris on the house phone.

'There's one in New York, apparently.'

'A zen one?'

'Apparently. I could run up on the train and bring her back.'

'A her? Not some horrible bimbo?'

'I doubt it. I'll find out.'

'Couldn't you call?'

'She doesn't have a phone. It's against her religion.'

Iris sounded dubious. 'I don't know what my daughter would say. She's getting a massage right now.'

'I know. Better not disturb her.' I hung up and was headed for freedom when I remembered my grand. It meant a long crawl up and down, and the risk of running into a setback, but I never liked to leave it in my room.

Love waited patiently. Clarence hovered. I got back feeling better and we headed for the train station.

It was a cold day, colder than ever. On the platform we stamped our feet, waiting for the Amtrak. When it pulled in we climbed on board. We were ready for the train's steam-heat, but it wasn't functioning. Love and I huddled in our window seats. The conductor hurried through the long compartment, blowing on his hands.

I stared out as white Pennsylvania gave way to white New Jersey. I found myself confessing long pent-up feelings of domestic distress to the parapsychologist of soul.

'She's living with her mother, who's always been against me. There's this guy hanging around.'

'Thass bad, British.'

'A lot of it's to do with money.'

'This dude's got it and you don't?'

'Her mother thinks he's a better bet than me. Always did.'

'She's some kinda grand lady, right?'

'She's called Lady Roxbury.'

'Lay dee Rox berry.' Love rolled the name around with relish. 'Man, she be livin' in a big ole castle, I bet.'

'Sort of. It's called Battle Manor. In Sussex.'

'Battle, ooee, thass the word all right. Brother, you better get yourself some *bread*.'

I was stung enough to pull out my grand. 'Look at this! I'm not completely broke. We'll have ourselves some fun.'

Love looked at the money and shook his head. 'Uh-huh. Fun ain't what we headed for, little brother. I think you better give that to me.'

'Give it to *you*?' I couldn't believe it.

Love was serious. 'You got a way of losin' it that just ain't healthy.' He tapped his nose. 'Doctor Love know a real investment. Pay a *handsome* dividend for you. Somethin' you *need*.'

I'd come by Fong's windfall so easily, so unexpectedly, I'd never really counted it as mine. And there was something in the good Doctor's eye, some mystical street-wisdom beyond my ken that put me in his power and convinced me. I was shocked at myself, all the same, as I handed the money over. Doctor Love buttoned the bundle away, with a knowing smile.

We passed through the marble magnificence of New York's Penn Station, and onto the blaring, honking, filthy street. It felt good. There was a charge in the air, so different to Philadelphia. I felt anything was possible again. The wind came down the cross-streets like knives, but even the cold here acted like a stimulant.

It was only a few blocks to where Doctor Love had stashed his gypsy cab. I spotted the bumper-sticker down the street, PARADOXICAL GENETIC INFUSION.

I guessed *where* we were headed as we howled over the Brooklyn Bridge, but I still didn't know *why*. Love was blandly intent on driving, drumming his fingers to some funky rhythms which killed conversation. Below us the Hudson was grey and choppy. A few boats battled through the white-caps. Steel suspension struts towered either side of us like a canyon.

Through the rear window the Manhattan skyline loomed, sprinkled with lit windows, windows yellow against the gun-metal daylight.

Something was different about the Galaxie Rollerdome. I knew it right away. We parked up the street. Love said, 'This is it. You ready?' The tension locked in. It was as if I was going back to school.

'What for?' My voice came small and weak.

Love nodded over at the entrance. Outside was a line of trucks: one bearing a big arclight, two that looked like mobile homes. 'Someone's makin' a *movie*.'

'Yes,' I said. 'My *God* . . .' I looked at Love wildly, then back down the street. As I did, someone came out and stood there, absently looking up and down at the traffic. My heart thumped. It was Henry Pelham.

'*Hey!*' I grabbed for the doorhandle and hit the street yelling his name. The traffic clattered by. Through it I saw his indifferent back disappearing into the doorway. I kept leaping off the sidewalk and back again, desperate to get across.

Love grabbed my arm. 'Hey, hey, hold on . . .!'

'*Bastards!*' I kept saying. '*Bastards!*'

'Hey! you ain't gettin' in there without a pass.'

Inside the Galaxie there were too many white faces. The face on the door was white. Love flashed his pass. 'This guy's with me.' I, too, was white, and it got me in.

Even the light was white, highlighting shabbiness in off-set areas. The magic mirrorball was still.

On-set were some familiar faces, black and white. Red-headed Lulu wore pink skating boots and a scantier version of her French maid's outfit, featuring suspenders and bare breasts framed in frilly lace. She showed only bored indifference to her toplessness, leaning up against Sammy Peach's director's chair, toying with the flower in his gangster jacket. Dotted about the set a selection of other beauties hung around, bare and bored.

I caught a flash from a familiar pair of glasses. Kenny leaned over to Sammy. Laughter floated across. Rojay and Mustaffa stood by, arms folded, sharing the joke.

I just wanted to get at them. Between me and the inner circle, equipment and technicians littered the floor. I had a clear enough run, save for Doctor Love, hanging onto my arm and counselling coolness.

Just then Henry reappeared, only feet away, coming out of the mensroom.

'*Hey*!' I yelled. This time he heard me. His lantern face lit into a smile. 'Shaw, you old bugger! What are *you* doing here?'

'You bastards! You've ripped me off!'

'Ripped you off? Steady on, old chap.'

'I won't steady on. I'll bloody kill you!'

Henry came closer, a look of concern on his face. 'You know, I really think you're serious.'

'Of course I'm bloody serious!'

'Calm down and tell me why you think you've been ripped off.'

'This is *my* film you're making. That's where I've been ripped off.'

'This picture isn't yours. This is Sammy's picture. He had the idea at that Sistine Chapel party of yours, after he met Lulu. She was the inspiration.'

I remembered Sammy and Henry whispering together. 'Then what are *you* doing here?'

'Well, as a matter of fact' – Henry looked coy – 'I don't necessarily want this broadcast, but I've got a certain amount of savvy in what you might call the porno market. I'm here as a sort of consultant.'

'But *I* told you all about this place, the whole rollerskating thing.'

'Rollerskating is as old hat as apple pie and Uncle Sam. Your idea was completely different to this, I remember. It was a sort of *Saturday Night Fever* thing. Straight boy-meets-girl stuff. This is porn on wheels. You wouldn't want to be associated with a thing like this.'

'I'd like to be associated with some money, that's what I'd like. I lost all mine selling this idea to Victor Ventura on yours and Kenny's advice. Now he tells me he's got a part in this.'

'Only a cameo part. He's got a heart condition, remember?'

I shook my head in frustration and despair. 'It just doesn't make sense.'

'Of course it doesn't make sense, old chap.' Henry cautiously kneaded my shoulder. 'If you want things to make sense, stay out of the movies.'

I shook him off. 'Fuck you, Henry! I'll tell you what does make sense, you bastard, what does make sense is I've been *ripped off*!'

Henry shrugged, 'If you really feel that way, old chap, you'd better speak to Kenny. He's the boss.'

In the hot glare of fantasy and face-paint I approached the boss on surreal feet. Everything around me seemed like freeze-frame, save for him. His glasses twinkled up at one of his starlets. I could see goose-bumps on her breasts.

The glasses blazed as he turned towards me, becoming dimly aware.

'*Hey!*' I was still wearing my uniform.

He looked baffled. 'What is it, Paul? I didn't send for you, did I?'

'No, Sir, you didn't *send* for me. I came on my own, dammit!'

He shook his head. 'I don't understand. Why are you here? Did Mrs Graumann – ?'

'This is *my film* you're making.'

'*Your* film?' Kenny turned to Sammy, laughing. 'I knew it was lousy. You didn't tell me it was written by a domestic.'

Sammy shrugged, laughing too. 'Why not? He shakes a pretty good cocktail.'

Lulu said, 'Hi, Paul. How the hell are you?'

'Sick, if you want to know. Sick of being ripped off by a lot of crooks and assholes.'

Kenny twisted around in his chair. 'Will someone get this shmuck outa here?'

'I'm not going,' I screamed, 'not until you give me satisfaction!'

Kenny said, 'Oh, yeah?' Two burly crew-members appeared in my pool of light.

'Ya wanna make pictures, fine. Do it on your own time, not on mine. You're *fired*!'

My voice came down from the rafters as I was hauled away. 'I'll get you, you bastards! You cheap fucking bastards! *You just see if I don't*!'

Back out on the street I sat on the sidewalk where I'd been dumped. Doctor Love looked down at me, nodding, with folded arms. 'That was cool.'

I looked back up at him, my eyes still hot. 'Well, what did you expect me to do?'

Love considered. 'Somethin' like that, I guess.'

'I'm glad you told me, Love. Yes, I'm *glad*. I'm glad I said all the things I said.'

'Me too, British. All the brothers sure *enjoyed* your act.'

I grinned and started to clamber to my feet. As I did so my two old friends the fat-wheel bikers appeared in the entrance.

'Hey, British, whass goin' on?'

I said, 'You may well ask.'

'We in the movies now, jes like you said we'd be.'

I returned to Philadelphia. On the dark journey I had time to reflect. I didn't see how I could continue working for a man who had cheated me. I had train fare but that was about it. Doctor Love had my only money in the world. His planned investment was now my only ray of hope. It wasn't much of one. His parting advice to me had been to keep the faith, but it wasn't easy. I was out of a job and without prospects. The likelihood of a glowing reference from Kenny Graumann was remote. I doubted whether my conduct would meet with much sympathy at home, when the awful moment inevitably came to tell them. Nor would it meet with much among certain ladies at the Grosvenor Hotel, I mused ruefully, as the train at last pulled in.

It was nine when I got to my room. It seemed a lifetime since I'd left it. There was a note under my door from Iris: *Call me*. I called her. Moments later she was in my room. She had removed her 'face' for the night and wore a lilac housecoat. She looked old and tired. Her dark eyes were deep pools of reproach.

'Honey, how *could* you?'

I sat on the edge of my bed, equally old and tired, and shook my head.

'My daughter is too upset to see you. She asked me to . . .'

I looked up, 'Asked you to?'

'Honey, she *needs* you, you know that. But she has to let you go this time.'

'Of course she does.'

'She's too upset to say goodbye.'

'I understand.'

'She asked me to give you this.' Iris looked embarrassed as she handed over a hundred-dollar bill.

I folded it away. 'Thanks.'

'To tide you over.'

'Please thank her very much indeed.'

Iris's mood abruptly changed. 'How could you *do* something like that, you klutz? You had it made.'

'He *swindled* me, dammit!' Somewhere a little angry energy remained.

'Swindled schmindled. He does it to everybody. He doesn't even *know* he's doing it. Why take it so personal?'

'Oh, I don't know.' I was too tired to feel much conviction about anything. 'What's the use talking about it? It's too late now.'

'You were the best butler in town, you jerk. Now no one'll hire you.'

'I suppose not.'

'Mr and Mrs Graumann will never give you a reference, not after those things you said.'

We said goodnight and goodbye. At the door Iris turned with an after-thought.

'You can stay here tonight, honey, but be out of the room early in the morning. No point making things worse.'

This remark injected my tiredness with acute apprehension. I thought I'd hit bottom, but in fact there was a place beneath. I was stranded and homeless and friendless and broke, staying on borrowed time in a den of enemies.

I knew only two people in New York. One of them, so far as I knew, didn't have a number. The chances of the other being there at this time of year were remote. I dug out my wallet from the bottom of my half-packed case. The little piece of paper was still there. I dialled direct, wondering as I did so whether instructions had yet been given to stop my calls. Apparently they hadn't. I listened to the ringing tone with mounting anxiety. Could he possibly be there? With a dozen homes to choose from I doubted it.

'Hallo?'

'Jimmy?' I gasped.

'Who's that?' He sounded irritable.

'It's Paul.'

'What's up, Paul?' He was incurious as ever.

'I didn't think you'd be there.'

'I only came by to pick up my new scuba stuff. I'm leaving town in the morning.'

'I don't suppose I could stay there for a few days, could I, Jimmy? I'm in a bit of a fix.'

'How many days?'

'Not too many.'

His mind on Bermuda sun, he couldn't be bothered to quibble. 'I'll leave the keys at the bistro,' he said grudgingly.

'Thanks Jimmy. Thanks a *lot*.'

I finished packing and went to bed, ready for an early start.

When the telephone rang it dragged me from a deep abyss of exhausted sleep. The digital clock said 0219.

I grabbed the phone, dropped it, retrieved it. 'Wha — ?'

A breezy southern accent floated down the wire. 'Room service . . .'

'Suzanne?'

'Ya want sump'n real special?'

'How did you know I was here?'

'Li'l ole bird told me.'

'Where are you?'

'Noo York.'

'Not downstairs?' I found myself laughing.

'No *siree*.'

'I'm in *deep* shit.'

'Heard that too.'

'News travels fast.'

'When it's bad it does.'

'I'm coming to New York.'

'Free for lunch?'

'I'm free for the rest of my life.'

'Where?'

I couldn't think. 'There's a bistro on Wooster and Spring. The Good Apple.'

'Sounds borin'.'

'Sure. One o'clock?'

'One, hun.' And she hung up.

By the time I got to SoHo Suzanne was already there — I could tell from the top of the street. Outside the Good Apple the big black limo shone outlandishly in the bright winter sun. Laid-back locals peered reluctantly at the blank, blacked-out windows. I carried my heavy bag down the slope from Broadway, not half as depressed as I might have been.

Inside, the scrub-faced waitresses leaned defensively against the backs of bentwood chairs, their wholesomeness under heavy pressure from the luncher at centre stage.

Suzanne was in full uptown battle order. Many ropes of pearls filled the gaps left by her Chanel suit. More pearls tied up her honey hair.

'Ah jus bin tellin' these here Yankee babes a thang or two about banana daiquiris.'

I dumped my bag and kissed her. Her mouth was cold and sweet. The Yankee babes shifted uneasily.

'Mmmm. I think I'd like one of those.'

'We made a jugful, didn't we, girls?'

We got through the jugful. We ate radicchio salads with raspberry wine vinegar dressing, followed by cold Maine lobsters. Suzanne ordered champagne and showed the girls how to pour it over fresh raspberries and cassis.

I said, 'So who was this little bird, exactly? I'm curious.'

'He's kind of a big bird, actually. A big, black bird.'

'Not by any chance a parapsychologist of soul?'

'That's the one, hun.'

One of the apple-cheekers hadn't minded popping round the corner for some strawberry shortcake. I grinned largely through a mouthful before washing it down. 'You've been hanging around roller-rinks, then?'

'Most nice girls where I come from lost their virginity in a roller-rink.' Suzanne had a loud voice. 'Anyways, that set belongs to ma boyfriend.' The wholesome girls put their heads down and got busy with other lunchers.

'Good lord!'

'Have you forgotten whose hard-earned dollars are paying for that dog of a movie?'

'Of course! I mean, I had, I suppose. It's all been so . . . bewildering.'

'We talked about your little problem, my boyfriend and I.'

'Oh, yes?'

'Domingo's a pretty straight guy in some ways. He liked

you. He thinks those sleazebags treated you wrong.'

'Bastards!' I frowned into my champagne-sodden raspberries.

'Don't you fret, darlin',' (Suzanne's cool hand on my wrist) 'he's makin' sure they give you points on the deal. If the thing's a hit, why, you'll be a millionaire!'

I smiled at her rather glumly. 'Not much hope of that, I'm afraid.'

'You never can tell. Gotta stay positive.' Her attention seemed to wander. After a few moments she said, 'Where are you stayin', exactly?' I felt a beat of excitement. With her sunny face, flushed with wine, she was almost impossibly beautiful.

'Just up there.' I pointed up to Jimmy's loft. There was a tightness to my voice. 'Why, coming up?'

'Are you crazy!' She flushed surprisingly, childishly red. She looked nervously at the door. 'The chauffeur in that car, he'd . . . he keeps a real careful eye on me.' She pulled herself together. 'Domingo and I, we got you a Christmas present, that's all. It's kinda big. You couldn't carry it too far . . .'

'You really are a terrific girl, Suzanne.'

I was shocked to see tears in her eyes. 'Hell, this is stoopid. It's a goodbye present too, Paul. Has to be.' I took her hand. She looked me full in the face. Her eyes were bright and wet. 'You don't know what you've done to me, you jerk.' Then she started laughing.

We walked out to the limo, not holding hands. The driver erupted from the front and dived into the back. He reappeared with a huge box that hardly fitted through the door. It was wrapped in red-and-gold paper, with a giant blue bow.

'My God, Suzanne. It *is* big!'

'Merry Christmas! You think you can manage?'

'Sure. It's only up there.' I glanced up, then back at the chauffeur. Suzanne held out her hand. I took it in mine, tried to think of something polite-sounding. 'Well . . . bye bye, then. And thanks.'

Suzanne took her hand away and turned to the car. The

chauffeur stood by the door, holding it stiffly open. As she stooped to enter she turned her face to me, away from him. She gave me a funny little strained smile. 'Y'all take care now, hear?'

It certainly was big. There were no lifts to the lofts. I got it up to Jimmy's somehow, along with my case. Once inside I opened some windows and leaned out, listening to the city. It sounded good. It was a bright, blowy, breezy day. Like a holiday. SoHo has a holiday feeling, most of the time. I turned to my gift.

I sat on the floor beside the giant box, and carefully removed the bow. It had a richness and complexity that should surely be preserved. Next I detached the lavish wrapping paper, just as slowly. My poverty was making me careful about waste. I opened the box and pulled out a lot of packing paper. It piled up around me. I reached another box. This one was sealed tightly with Sellotape. I wrestled with it, cursing all practical jokers. When I finally got inside it I was greeted by a thick layer of straw. Burying my hands in the straw, I could feel something bulgy and crumply at its heart. A thick manilla envelope was stuffed to bursting point with what I could feel was more paper. Sitting on the littered floor I laughed, 'Oh, God, Suzanne. What a crazy girl you are.' I took it by the top in my two hands and ripped it open. The air filled with money.

Later on, the warehouse windows framed violet light like paintings. Evening was falling. It had taken me all afternoon to gather up the cloud of bills and count them. They were all hundreds, in various stages of falling apart. Organising them in piles helped keep me from falling apart myself. I did a re-count but it didn't make any difference. There were a thousand of them.

In the end I stuffed them into a pillowcase and sat there next to them on the sofa, staring out of the window, occasionally crumpling them with my hand. I thought of all the different things I could do. I was paralysed.

I was jerked from my reverie by a heavy banging on the door. Doorbells aren't quite funky enough for lofts. I reacted immediately with panic. Piling a beanbag on top of my fortune I yelled, 'Who's there?!'

'Airport cab, boss.'

'I didn't order any airport cab.'

'This the address I got.'

There was something about that voice. I walked across to the door, still paranoid, put my ear to the steel. I thought I could hear muffled whispers.

'Not a *gypsy* cab, is it?'

'Open up and find out, honky.'

Doctor Love stood in the doorway, holding a bag. There was something familiar about the bag. I couldn't quite place it. I looked up at the big stupid grin on his face. It almost split his head in half.

'Guess who I picked up at the airport today, British?'

She moved out from behind him. She looked thin and pale and her wild hair was everywhere. She wore old jeans and an old sweater. The small bulge of her breasts quickened my pulse immediately.

'Hi, Paul.' Her voice sounded small and strained.

'Natasha!' I looked helplessly at Love, shaking my head. 'I don't understand . . .'

'This guy sent me a ticket . . .'

'A First Class Ticket,' Doctor Love said proudly.

'First class, yes.' There were bright spots on Natasha's cheeks. 'It was great.'

Love said, 'I told you I had a good investment for you. Something you *need*.' I looked at Natasha. I could hardly breathe.

She said, 'We got a message at home. Something terribly important. I've been worried sick.'

Love said, 'I told her. No need to worry. She won't listen.'

Natasha was getting mad. 'I just want to know what's going *on*!'

I shook my head. 'You're right, Love. She never listens.'

'God, Paul . . .'

'Well,' Love gave the high sign from the door, 'I'm going to leave you folks to get acquainted.'

I said, 'Hold on, Doctor Love, I . . .' But he was gone, banging the heavy door shut. I heard his sneakers squeaking down the stairs.

I turned to Natasha. Her face had a chilly look. I moved towards her. She moved away. 'This place is OK.'

I said, 'It's Jimmy's.'

'What's been going on, Paul?' She stood staring at the mass of wrapping debris.

I didn't answer. I was looking out of the window. Doctor Love's gypsy cab sashayed up the street towards Broadway. I could still read the bumper-sticker: PARADOXICAL GENETIC INFUSION.

Natasha had moved near the sofa, right in front of the beanbag. I went over to her, without hesitation, and pushed her down. She looked angry and rattled. I jumped on top of her, squashing her into the crunchy beans. She tried to struggle up. 'Come on, Paul . . .'

I had my hands up her sweater. She wasn't wearing anything underneath. I squeezed both her breasts and pushed my mouth down roughly onto hers. She pulled away. I could feel her shivering. 'I want to know what's so important.'

'You're sitting on it.' I tugged up her sweater and started pulling it over her head.

'Get off me, you bastard!' But the sweater was off and my hands were at the waist of her jeans.

'Are you *mad*?'

'*Yes!*' I got the top stud undone, dragged down on the zip. It moved an inch or two. I gripped both sides of the waistband and pulled. At last I felt her shift herself slightly, so they came down more easily. She said, 'Supposing someone comes in?'

I said, 'Don't worry, Natasha, it's OK. Everything's OK.'

I looked down at the amazing concave whiteness of her belly

and hips. Her panties had rolled down with her jeans, revealing the dark, magic delta. Her hands were on me too, now, cool and hard. There was no control. I put my mouth to her ear, buried my face in her gypsy hair, whispered, ' "Between the longing for love, and the fight for the legal tender . . ." '

'What?' Her face was suffused, melting.

'It's a quote. Jackson Browne. I couldn't help thinking of it.'

'God, Paul, can't you *ever* stop quoting?'

Paul couldn't explain for a while, though the greenbacks crackled occasionally. Later, when he did, Natasha was very, very happy.